being small

chaz brenchley

per ✷ *Aspera*

Edited by Shannon Page
Cover art by Mark J. Ferrari
Published by Per Aspera Press
www.perasperapress.com

ISBN   978-1-941662-01-4 (tradepaper)

Library of Congress Cataloging-in-Publication Data

Brenchley, Chaz, author.
  Being Small / by Chaz Brenchley.
      pages cm
    ISBN 978-1-941662-00-7 (hardcover) -- ISBN 978-1-941662-01-4
(tradepaper)
    I. Title.
    PR6052.R38B45 2014
    823'.914--dc23
                                        2014019802

First printing: August 2014

praise for chaz brenchley

"Brenchley worms his way into the heads and
hearts of his characters and tells their terrible,
tragic truths…an assured and accomplished
story-teller at the peak of his powers."
VAL McDERMID, Tangled Web

"The prose is impeccable…"
ELIZABETH BEAR, *Realms of Fantasy*

"…a lean novel with heavy themes, lyrical
narration about harsh reality…Brenchley's
haunting characters feel like real people
making real choices…"
MINDY KLASKY, bestselling author of the Glasswright series

"…a powerful, moving book that will haunt me
a long, long time."
JAIME LEE MOYER, award-winning author of *Delia's Shadow*

"*Being Small* is brilliantly creepy, too true to life
to be full-blown horror, but deeply disturbing
none the less…Highly recommended!"
KATHARINE KERR, author of The Deverry Cycle

This is for everyone
I ever disappointed.

Sorry. Just not big enough.

— M M, Oxford, '03

I

CALCULUS

To-day I playd my brother is a live.
I told mum. She said reely. And how did he
feel abowt it.
I said he wosn hapy.

. . .

It's strange how swift, how keen we are to give ourselves away. I was, what, four years old? Five, perhaps.
No more than that. And being precocious, keeping my
first diary in the back of a discarded Moleskine notebook
of my mother's. I didn't think to date it, and there are no
reference-points to fix it anywhere in time; I suppose I
could ask her, but I doubt if she would help. I doubt she
could. One notebook among dozens, hundreds maybe,
and she never dated them either. No telling whether this
one had been abandoned the week before I started using
it, the month before, the year before or longer.

It doesn't matter, anyway. The text, that's what's important, not the date. I was burning-bright, I was blazingly impatient, I couldn't bear to have the urgency of my thoughts dragged down to the slow tempo of orthography, of asking one word after another how each was spelled. Anything above four letters I hadn't learned yet, so I went for the phonetic option and wrote by ear.

Anything except. At that age I could already spell brother. And I understood my brother too, more than just in embryo. That's textual, it's there, you can read it. I was exact in saying that he wouldn't have liked my pretending he was alive. He wasn't. He was dead, and that mattered to us both. He always had been dead; our whole relationship was predicated on the fact of it.

Which was why I wrote about it, first and early; why I'm still doing that, still at it, older and better-spelled but still struggling to make sense of it on paper, my life and my brother's other thing, his unlife, his being dead. Nothing changes.

Nothing ever changes. I still live by my brother's side, necessarily on my mother's back, you can't have one without the other. I still write for both of us and do it on her skin, on her 'Skines. She scatters, where I glean. She sketches on one side of the paper only, leaves whole pages blank and then abandons what she's made. I gather them up, these little black books, I hoard them all and write on the reverse, in all the blanks, I fill those bare white spaces. Profligacy, parsimony: she can't keep hold of what's important, and I can't let anything go. I'm only ever generous with words. Even then, my handwriting is — well, crabbed. Tight, held back, to make the most of all that open paper. Controlled or cramped or crushed; cabin'd, cribb'd, confin'd. What I'm trying not to say, since you ask, what I like never to say is that it's small.

· · ·

Small was my brother, where I was Michael. Always Michael, not Mike; neither Mikey, Mickey, Mick. I was never happy with contractions, and I hate diminutives. I had to do all the growing for both of us, for Small and me; of course I wasn't comfortable when people tried to make me smaller than I was. I worked for every inch of growth, I valued every letter of my name and wanted more, I wanted middle names and hyphens and increase.

My mother wouldn't give them to me, almost the only time that she was mean with what she could afford. "Small is Small and you are Michael, what do you need with other names, or more? Be who you are, boys, both of you, make the names worthy to contain you."

· · ·

There was a jar containing Small. She'd taken me to see it, just the once. Hand in hand on a Saturday morning, one of our expeditions: this one not up a college tower or down into the bowels of a museum, not a long walk among the river meadows or harder work to climb above the city, all the way up Shotover for a view of spires rising from a stony shadow, all the murk and sprawl of history in the keeping, in the making, in a broad and shallow bowl. This particular expedition took us, she took me to the station, to a train; and then half an hour later through streets that she knew and I didn't, another town, the echo of another life before me. Before us, I should say, before Small-and-me. Sometimes I could be selfish, though, it was easier back then. He was so much a part of me, I could forget that we were not in fact the same little boy, just me, hand in hand with my mother.

And so we came to an edifice, a monument, an example of Victorian engineering, social as much as structural: a red brick building with a frontage too long to see straight, far too long to have been built straight, all bows and bays half-hidden by the last of the English elms only waiting to be diseased. It was almost too high for me to see the top of it, standing too close with my little head tipped back almost far enough to topple me; and what I did see was fake, battlements that must be hiding the slate slopes of the roof, that were only there to top out the Gothic upthrust of the turrets.

I might have asked, "Where are we?" — but there were words cut into the stone arch above the iron-studded oak of the door, and they would tell me before my mother would. I was maybe six by now, and long words came easily to me. *Queen's College* needed only a blink, a moment of recognition, I'd seen that before; *School* was simple, basic, I knew several of those. I walked past them every day and never troubled my head with what went on inside. *Medicine* took a little subvocal work, a mental trip-and-recover before I knew it for the thing it was.

"What does it mean, a school of medicine?" I asked cheerfully enough, not expecting any useful answer, only really wanting to observe that I had read it all in the briskness of our passage up the steps to the doorway.

"School for grown-ups," she said, "it's where people learn to be doctors."

"Not us, though. We don't go to school." Unless she'd decided that should change, we should change again, her mind and my life. All our lives. That was always on the cards.

"No, darling. Only when they're useful. We're here to visit Small."

That needed thinking about. Small was in my head, in my heart, no longer in my belly nor in hers. And he was dead, of course, that was inherent. I didn't see how he could be here unless he'd come with us, or why we should bring him in order to visit him somewhere alien and enormous when I played with him daily in our own house, our own garden, all our private places.

It needed thinking about, but I wasn't given the time to think, nor spared the breath for questions. I was dragged clickety-click behind her sharp and bustling heels, down the corridor and up the stairs. Up many flights of stairs, where they wound themselves squarely around the open ironwork of a lift-shaft, and I thought she was denying me the breathless adventure of that lift simply to keep me out of breath and out of thinking.

Classic behaviour, perhaps, for a classic parent, to buy herself a lull from questions; but it wasn't like her. Questions were the point and purpose of the world, or of our being in it. That was why I didn't go to school, she'd explained that, so that we'd have more time to ask each other questions.

So I was questioning myself already in the heat of that yank-and-scurry, wondering what was different here or now: how we'd managed to leave Small behind in order to visit him here, and whether that meant we had to behave like normal people now, in that world where grown-ups had no time for children.

It seemed not, or not for long. Just a vagrant weakness slipping unregarded into my mother's head, shy as smoke and about as enduring. After the stairs came a corridor; halfway down the corridor was a door, one among dozens; she skittered her knuckles across its varnished panels in a vague pretence at knocking before she pushed it open and pulled me in, all without pause, all a part of that same long movement that had possessed us both since we entered the building.

She had, it occurred to me then, been here before.

And had met him before, the man behind the desk; and more to the point he had clearly met her, been expecting her, known at least a little of what to expect. This sudden irruption, curious woman and curious small boy, didn't faze him in the least. He rose to his feet already smiling, as if he understood already what some men took months to learn, what some men never learned at all.

"Mrs Martin. It's a pleasure to see you again," and it was, quite clearly, he was looking forward to spending this time with her. I beamed hotly. No swifter way to win my approval back then, than to show approval of my mother.

"So you're Michael," he said, looking down at me but not talking down and blessedly not reaching, not patting or tousling or going for one of those soft ridiculous all-men-together handshakes that I used to resent almost more than any other kind of condescension, "and you've come to see your brother."

I nodded, because that was what she'd said also. It still bewildered me. Grown-ups were strange as a matter of course, almost I thought as a matter of principle, but my mother could generally be relied on. Today I wasn't sure.

"Good. Well then, Michael, how do you want to do this? Shall I just bring him out, or do you want to talk about him first, what happened to him, to both of you, things like that?"

I shook my head, pleased to find that I could be so firm about it. What had happened to Small and me was a private affair, not to be discussed with strangers. This man might have walked a casual way into my affections by being so clearly pleased to see my mother; that didn't give him any right to share in family matters.

"Don't you even want to know what he's going to look like?"

Someone else's description, someone else's Small, what would be the point of that? I knew what Small looked like to me; I knew that no one else could see him the way that I did. I'd already figured out what this meant, that I could never see him as other people did. That may be a definition of sentience, that moment of realisation that your world is personal to you and nothing is universal, nothing is shared. It's certainly the font, the source of all loneliness.

We spend the rest of our lives in futile resistance: touching, grabbing, holding on grimly, making believe that the whole is greater than the sum of its parts when we know all along that it's a lie, we're lying to ourselves and to each other, to our children. Especially to our children, and sooner or later they will know it too. Me, I got there early. Being bright isn't always a blessing. Smart isn't always lucky. Just ask Small.

I shook my head again, and said, "When you show him to me, I will see."

He looked at me, and for a moment I knew what he was going to say. *Out of the mouths of babes and sucklings…* People were always doing that. I had my best scowl ready for the occasion, and I was all set to snap that I wasn't a babe and I hadn't suckled since I was three years old. There was no better weapon in my armoury, than making grown men flame with embarrassment in front of my mother.

But he looked at me and perhaps he saw the scowl building, perhaps he sensed the riposte waiting. Perhaps he was just a decent man who thought better of a lazy phrase. He said, "Quite right," and nothing more; and turned to a high cupboard set into the wall at his back, and opened the doors to show a rack of shelves, rows of great glass jars with strange contents. It was dark in there, within the shadow of the open doors. I thought it was meant to be, I thought all the lights in the room were arranged that way. And he was a broad-backed man and he stood four-square between me and the cupboard and I thought that was deliberate also.

A clever man, a decent man, he was a careful man as well. He'd known that we were coming, he knew what we wanted, he knew just where it was and still he checked, he took a moment to bend close and read a label in that darkness before he lifted out one of the jars and set it down on his desk, in the light.

A glass jar, the height of a man's forearm, the breadth of a man's hand from fingertip to wrist. Straight-sided, round: even empty it would have said *laboratory* rather than *sweetshop*, even to me who had never seen a lab.

It wasn't empty, but I wasn't ready yet to look at what it held. Not directly, not gazing in through glass at what might be gazing back at me.

The lid of the jar was shaped to give a grip, but not for carrying. He'd lifted it down two-handed, handled it as if it was heavy as well as precious. Probably it was.

Nor was that lid coming off in a hurry. I could see tape wrapped around the join to seal it. Only a precaution against spillage, obviously. I wasn't young enough to think that they needed bindings to keep Small in, to stop him clambering out. I don't believe I ever had been young enough for that. How could they contain him, in a jar or anywhere? Small was mine, with me, inside me and around. He always had been.

· · ·

Here in the jar, though, he was something entirely other. He was a dough-boy and I thought he was swimming, the way he dandled in the water, arms wide and eyes open. I thought there would be bubbles leaking from his mouth at any moment. I looked to see him wave.

• • •

Well, no. He wasn't, I didn't. None of that. It was only a moment, an image in an eye-blink, not long enough for the thoughts to form. I leaned forward, bent right over the desk to see better; my hands did their own thing, reaching out to clutch the cool curve of the glass, maybe tugging just a little at the weight of it, to slide it just an inch across the wood.

My mother spoke my name: a caution, a warning, whatever. It didn't matter.

• • •

Seen close, he was more like porridge than dough. Porridge a day old, skinned over. Lumpy porridge, where the lumps show through the grey slip of the skin. And he was squat, bulbous, only crudely human: toad-creature, troll-baby, seeming to smile wide and happy and nub-toothed in his bath.

And he was my brother, my twin and part of me, as I was part of my mother: one sundered flesh, twice sundered. I could feel the scar on my belly where the edge of the desk was pressing my waist as I pivoted across it, on tiptoe and far astretch.

I'd never had to reach so far for Small. I'd never felt so distant. That glass, that glassy stare, little black eyes in folds of pasty flesh, uncooked pastry was closer almost than porridge and the way his hands were lifted, perhaps to keep me out, to thrust me back — this might have been a worry for my mother. Not the same worry that the man had, the custodian of the jars, that the sight of what he kept in custody might scare or sicken or disturb me. Even playing at being a normal parent, she couldn't take the game that far. But she might have worried that this fat and floating gnome, this lardy-boy could squeeze Small out of my mind, out of my life, that I would lose my long-time companion in this vision of a stunted thing, a dead thing, O my brother...

She might have agonised over that, for my sake and her own. But she was always bold, my mother, and leaving things undone was never one of her sins. If there was something for me to see, I would be shown it. If Small was there to be visited, we would visit, and whatever price to pay, we could face that later.

She knew me better than she thought she did, or else she had wasted a whole lot of worry. Now that I had seen, I understood exactly, and nothing in my world was shaken. I nearly turned to Small at my side to explain it to him, to be sure that he was keeping up: *this is your body that was cut out of me, because you were growing inside me where you shouldn't have been; and look how funny your hair was, just those long little wisps like a troll, and you were growing fat on my food, you can see that, what a pudge you were, and I was so skinny, we've seen the photos, remember? That's how they knew you were there, because of the lump you made in my belly. So you had to come out, and it's been ever so better since for both of us, although you died; you had to be dead but that's never mattered and they kept your body, see, and this is it. Oh, look, fingernails...*

· · ·

Only that once, we ever went to see him. It was interesting for all of us, but there wasn't any point in going back. He wouldn't have changed at all, bobbing about in his jar there, and change is what matters. Growing out of your clothes, growing into your life, chasing difference. Like this:

I want to be older, bigger, smarter, happier. I want to be an orphan, I want to be a cat. I want to learn to ride my bike. I want to be that boy's friend, or that boy's. I want to be somebody's friend. I want a television in the house. I want a television in my bedroom. I want to go to school and get a new haircut and another pair of shoes, I really want to want those sorts of things...

II

BEING SMALL

What can he say, what can he do...?

He squats in my shadow, in my pocket, in my mind's eye. He rides my shoulders like a cat with all its claws out. He is the monkey on my back, but he ain't heavy, he's my brother. No dead weight.

His name isn't necessarily his description, it depends how you're looking at him at the time. What time of day it is when you're looking, what year it is, how old we are, like that. Like a shadow, he grows as I grow. Like a shadow he grows and shrinks, stretches and collapses and stretches again as the light shifts, as it changes. He never changes, though. Of course he doesn't. He can't, he's dead. I change, all the time I change; he stays the same, the same as me, identical.

All through my childhood, he is my unimagined friend. He does those things that imaginary friends most famously will do, only Small does them all for real. Constant companion, familiar as an old scar, he shares my

games, my dreams, my bookshelves, my wardrobe and my
bed. He'd share my friends too, surely, if I had any. He
reads over my shoulder, he follows in my footsteps, he
leads me far astray. Reliable as a squashed and sour bear,
comfortable as a bed of nettles, he laughs at me, cries for
me, whispers to me like an aching tooth. The only thing
he can't do is die alongside me, any of our games that call
for dying. He's been there already, he's dead and you never
can go back for a second try at that. Not allowed. One
time pays for all, with no returns.

How I see us then, we're always running: uphill to the
park, my voice shrill in the chill of an Oxford morning.
People stare at me in the street, thinking me mad, thinking I'm shrieking at myself. They're wrong, and they can't
know it, never will — he is not me, how could he be? and
where's solipsism when you need it? — so they'll always
think they saw a mad boy in his fever, ducking his own
shadow, unaware. But I never can keep Small bottled
up. That's someone else's job. I know that, I have seen. It
frees me, perhaps, a little; perhaps it frees us both. If the
haunted, the married, twinned souls ever can be free.

I don't feel haunted, nor married. Not then. Neither
free. I feel avid, immediate, observed. As though I have
to live for both of us, at double speed. Have I read *1984*
yet, or has my mother read it to me? Almost certainly one,
and maybe both. I know Little Brother is watching me, I
always have known that; but the sense I have that the big
man in the novel is floating, bobbing, passively watching,
having his people accumulate experience on his behalf
while he lies back and soaks it up like a sponge in water,

that's got to date from this time, round about. It can't be retrospective.

Whether this really is what Small wants, what he wants to watch, all this dashing about, conspicuous consumption — well, that's another question and you'd probably have to ask him. Not that I'd ever trust the answer. Who can tell, in the end, what any other person ever wants?

Who can ever tell what he wants himself, come to that?

III

CHAOS THEORY

I want a home that doesn't move, *that doesn't move and move and move again. I want my own hat-peg in my own house, I want never to move again. I want a mother who doesn't keep making me move. I want to go back to bed — to my bed, I want it to be my bed in my room, mine for keeps — and I want to curl up and pull the duvet over my head and listen to the radio under there and have a torch and read books and drink coke till I fart fizzy and never move at all, not ever again.*

The room was damp and the bed was spineless, saggy and full of creaks, and the mattress was being eaten away inside by its own springs, so that I had to use blu-tack to fix coins to the sharp points of them to stop them piercing me when I rolled over or stretched out. It was no bad room to be leaving, no great loss. I was twelve years old, I badly needed a bed that didn't creak.

And yet, and yet ...

I guess there comes a time when you want just to hold on to what's familiar. When the liquid rush of change turns acid, when it starts to dissolve your bones because they're the only solid thing left to you and you want to scream against the bite, the burn, the betrayal of it, and your mother's voice has just the same acidity as she says, "Honestly, Michael, I don't know why you're making all this fuss. I can't wait to be shot of this place, the old man with his halitosis and that dreadful hair. He was charging too much, anyway. We'll be much better off in the new house. We've got the whole attic to ourselves, and there's a shower in the box-room, practically en suite. That's better than sharing. We'll be better off all round. It's a nicer neighbourhood, there's a park, I'll find a job that pays more. We'll be happy, you'll see. So stop sulking, pick up that box and come along. Every time, we have this palaver. It's getting boring. You didn't want to move here six months ago, so why are you suddenly so keen to stay? It's not as if you'd made any friends around here. And you were right when we came, that room of yours does have a smell to it. I'd think you'd be glad to leave. Forget this place, shake the dust from your feet and move on. A child your age, you should always be keen to go. Stillness is stagnation. Think about waking tomorrow in a new bed..."

Which reminded me: I left the box on the stairs and darted back up to retrieve four two-pence coins from their precarious balance in the body of the mattress, poised like spinning plates on poles to save my poor sore skin from further punctures. I worked the blu-tack off them with my thumb as I clumped heavily down again, and played with it like a bogey in my hand all the way to the new house.

• • •

New house, new room, new bed. New view, night and morning. It was light and air and music to my mother, not to me. I ached for permanence, for roots. Sometimes I longed to be discovered by social workers, seized in a dawn raid, taken into care for my own wellbeing. Locks on the doors and a watch kept at night, I'd like that. Or I thought about being picked up for shoplifting, held on remand; it was easy enough to get caught, surely. And when they saw how feckless my mother was, how unreliable, how unlikely to surrender me for trial — well, they couldn't conceivably let me go. It would be custody or nothing. Somewhere strong and stern and Victorian for preference, barred windows and high walls. Secure accommodation. That was what I wanted, more than anything. I wanted to see a full four seasons through the same pane of glass. And my mother wouldn't have it: *stale* she said, *dull, bourgeois* she said when she wasn't saying *peasant*. Stability was death, she said; if you were sitting still you might as well stop breathing. Roots? Just look at roots, she said. Pale and limp and insipid, growing downwards, always down into the dark to sip sour liquids from a matrix enriched with rot.

Look at Small, she might have said, *dead and still in his jar, floating in formalin, pickled and preserved. Now that's stability for you. Is that what you want?*

She never did say that, of course not; but it was sub-text, it was there. Maybe that's why she rushed me on so often and so fast, because I had to rush for both her boys. But I knew that already, I was doing it every way I could. Sometimes I felt I was sprinting ahead — calculus, chaos theory, carbon dating, bring it on — and leaving them both behind, my mother and Small together, doubling the distance between us every day. Sometimes I felt all my brother's weight on my shoulders — Japanese, Judaica, James Joyce — and I was ready to stumble any step now, trying to carry the both of us and her expectations too. He ain't heavy, no, but she could make him seem so.

And always, always she made him the excuse for this motility, the constant cycle from Banbury Road to Cowley Road, from Jericho to Hinksey as though we were nomads following the grass, or planetoids in an unstable orbit around the gravitational hub that was intellectual Oxford. Never too close — she had a job in Bodley for a while, but not a long while — and never ever breaking far away. "If you want to move," I said to her more than once, often, time and again, "why don't we move properly, why don't we go and live somewhere else?"

She cited the advantages of a university city, and I said that there were others. She mentioned her graduate status here and the access that it gave her, that she could use on my behalf; I pointed out that she never did use it, on my behalf or her own or anyone's else. But at least it's there, she said, it's a facility. Potential educative energy, she said, stored and available, like nowhere else on Earth. Even the brickwork has gravitas, she said, learning is osmotic; just brush your fingers along the college walls and feel the tingle of it, feel the bite. We can't leave here, she said, you were born here, you were born for this. Both of you, she said. Living in Oxford, she said, it's like being annealed with knowledge, every day a passing through the furnace. You wouldn't be so wise, she said, if you hadn't done your growing here.

I said but I had, I'd been here and done that and maybe it was time to let me cool off somewhere else. She said I was still —

And then she checked herself, on the very edge of saying entirely the wrong word; and stumbled almost as she turned the sense around and called me not so big yet, said I had room for a lot more growing.

All of which meant that we weren't going anywhere, except round and round again in our private endless trek, the pursuit of something unattainable. Didn't matter what it was that we pursued, I sometimes thought, so long as it was guaranteed to keep out of reach, to keep us reaching. My mother might name it excellence, or betterment, or learning — except that she never learned, nothing ever got better and the only thing we excelled at was being ourselves, our own spectacular conceit.

. . .

Like this:

New house, new street. Back to North Oxford, big Victorian houses and mature trees, shadow and substance both at once; land of dons and little businesses, ditto ditto. Our landlady was a crispy little woman who had inherited both the house and the business that had bought it, a small textile company. She rented out her attic floor not for the money, which she didn't need — which was why we could afford to live there, because she had let my mother batter her down far and far from a commercial rent, because she didn't care — and not for the company, which she didn't want. We had a key to the main door, but were encouraged not to use it. Our way in and out was the iron fire escape that clung to the back wall and climbed among the ivy. As near as I could work it out, Mrs Tilson took in lodgers out of a general principle, because she was a single woman in a large house with more space than she could possibly require. I'm sure she took in us specifically because my mother leaned on that principle, with all the significant weight that she could muster: a single mother with a part-time job, a boy on the near edge of adolescence, both greatly in need of better quarters than they could afford on the open market.

Being entirely unprincipled herself, she'd have done that as a matter of habit. And once we were in, of course she reached for more. The room on the half-landing below our floor, not used except for storage, what a school-room it would make, now that I needed space to that degree. And textiles meant off-cuts, and my mother could do so much with off-cuts, run up bags and belts and little fabric gifts to sell at market, for the money my education so sorely needed...

· · ·

All of that and more and too much more, but I took comfort from it. It took time, she invested time in squeezing poor little Mrs T who thought herself so sharp, so brisk; and surely she wouldn't waste what was so valuable to her, all that time, for the sake of a few short months in residence? Surely she must be thinking to stay this time, to hold on to what we had, so much better than we'd ever had before.

Almost, I let myself believe it. Absolutely, I let myself grow lazy, accepting, assuming.

· · ·

Like this:

"Hi."

"Hullo."

A boy with a bike, and just the low garden wall between us, that and a world of strange. We knew these conversations, Small and I. We were twelve years old, and we'd been having them all my life.

"You've just moved in."

"Last month, yes."

"I saw you."

He'd been watching, from his end of the street. I couldn't have known that unless we'd been watching him too, on and off all that month. He looked my age, he had a bike, we were the only boys visible in the immediate neighbourhood. We should gravitate by nature, at least for the little while that it took to learn if we were going to fling apart. I expected that. I was a pessimist by training and by experience; usually it needed only the one conversation. Perhaps I should learn to lie. I was sure my mother would teach me, and back me up where necessary, if the result was that I could buy or borrow or steal a friendship.

This boy was as cautious as I was, though. It had taken him a fortnight to coast casually past just at the time that I was out there and alone, unmothered, available. He'd had a dozen chances already, and let them all go by. I liked that. So no, no lying. Let it happen, and let it be.

"What's your name, then?"

"Michael. And you're Adam."

"How d'you know that?"

"It's painted on your bike." On the frame, in blue capitals, very uncool.

"Oh. Yeah. My dad's idea. It's got the postcode on the other side. He thinks that'll stop it being nicked." Adam thought it was a humiliation, clearly.

I grunted, with that kind of tempered sympathy that becomes a speciality after a lifetime, even a short lifetime of always being worse off than everyone else. *That's too bad, but* starts off as a phrase, becomes a tone of voice, eventually just a cough. "You should see mine. No one would want to nick it." Certainly no one would want to ride it. Only my mother could ever imagine that anyone might, that I might. We lived in a bubble, yes, but I could still see out.

"Yeah? So what is it, then?"

"I don't think it's got a name. I don't think it ever had a name. It's just a bike." It had adjectives — generic, geriatric, decrepit, disused — but none that could qualify even as description. I was angling noisily for a dog just then, and that was just my excuse for walking everywhere. *See how much walking I do? Of course I need a dog.* Truth worked the other way: I wanted the dog to give me the excuse to walk, not to have to ride my bike.

"Let's see."

Nothing I could do, once he'd asked. I went to fetch the thing from where I kept it beneath the fire-escape, cloaked in a tarpaulin, "against the weather" was what I said to Mum. Adam sucked air through his teeth, and clearly felt much better about his own embarrassing machine.

"It's too small for you, though. Haven't you got a little brother you could pass it on to?"

Here we go. Round the mulberry bush, round and round again. "Yes and no," I said, still not good at lying, never having had the chance to learn. "I've got a brother, he's Small, he's my twin, but he can't ride a bike."

"Why not?"

"He's dead."

A blink, a shuffle, a glance aside; a curious look back. "I'm sorry. That's awful. When did he … ?"

The real question was *how did he … ?* This was old ground, familiar ground, and I'd never really cared. Of course they wanted to know, who wouldn't? And Small was mine, his life had been mine and his death was

intimately my own and I could afford to be generous with
the news of it. No boy's gossip could diminish me, or us.

"Oh, he's always been dead, he was born dead, almost.
He was born out of me, and then he died. In my arms, but
I was asleep, I don't remember that." Except in dreaming,
and maybe the dreams were only what my mother told me.

"I don't..."

Didn't understand, didn't believe? Of course he didn't.
Who would, a chance-met boy with a fable running counter to all biology lessons, all the sweat and slime of the TV
documentaries, all the grunts and whispers of his lying,
lubricious, ignorant, studious friends? But it was a warm
day, a day for T-shirts and shorts. I pulled up the hem of
one and pushed down the waist-band of the other, and he
still couldn't see all the length of the finger-thick scar that
zipped my belly up.

"That's where they cut him out of me," I said. And
then, taking pity on his bewilderment, or else perhaps
valuing his obvious wish to believe me, "Look, we were
twins together, in my mother's womb, yeah? But very
early on, we'd already split into two but we sort of got
joined together again, and I just absorbed him into me. It
happens. Kind of like Siamese twins, only the weak one's
internal. He went on being himself, he even kept on growing, just very very slowly, and he took all his nutrition
out of me. That's why we call him Small, because we're
identical twins but he never got to be my size, or anything
near it. Big enough, though. That's how they knew he was
there, because of the lump he was making in my belly."

"What, you mean like a cancer?"

That was what they all said, it was a label they thought they understood. "Sort of. If a cancer could be like a person. Small started to show because I was so thin, because he drank all the strength out of me. That's like cancer. And they decided they had to cut him out of me, that's like cancer too, except that they knew he'd die if they did it, and that's like Siamese twins again, where they have to be separated but only one of them will survive. It's a moral dilemma."

"He wasn't a proper person, though. Er, was he ...?"

"He's my brother," I said flatly. "Why not?" I wasn't going to tell him about the little fat clean white grubby boy in the jar. My brother, the pickled twin. That kind of Small he might understand, where I still couldn't get my head around it. I didn't want anyone understanding my brother better than I did.

He shrugged, bony and awkward under the sun's weight. "So will you be coming to my school, then?"

"I don't go to school."

"You don't? Not ever?"

"No."

"Why not?"

"We never have. Mum teaches us at home."

His eyes narrowed, and I thought he was going to ask *you and who?* If I said *me and Small* I knew he'd figure out that jar, only he'd see it perched on a schooldesk next to me and he'd be off on his bike in a moment. I held my breath, and he asked a different question altogether.

"What, are you some kind of genius, then?"

Relief was a hard, high giggle in my throat, like

bubbles rising, bursting. "Me? I don't think so. My mother says not. That's why. She says that smart boys do okay wherever, but ordinary boys need special help, if they're going to be special."

He pulled a face, but it was fairly friendly. "What's it like?"

"Dunno, I've never done the other thing. What's school like?"

Another kind of face. "Holidays are better. Home-work's better, you can do that with the telly on. You're lucky."

I didn't feel lucky, I never had. I was meaning to explain that, but just then my mother appeared, saw us both with our bikes and sent us off. "That's good, Michael, that's the best idea. You two go riding and keep yourselves out of my hair. What's your friend's name, Adam, is it? Which number do you live at, Adam? Well, you take my Michael away and show him around, where's good for a bike and where's not. If you don't bring him back before teatime, you can have your tea with us..."

My mother is the original plague of locusts. Sometimes there's nothing you can do but run away.

· · ·

For a while there, everything made sense. And so, of course, inevitably, we came to this:

"Your mum's mad."

"This is news? Whoo, déjà vu. I know my mother's

mad. You know my mother's mad. You knew it the day we met."

"Yeah, but I thought mad in a good way. This is just crazy."

"Welcome to my life."

"I mean, you've got it made in that house, the old lady's practically paying you to live there. Why would she ever make you move?"

"Because she hates to see me happy?"

We both fell silent for a moment, giving that thought the space it deserved. Then we both sat up, turning away from it, from each other. I can't speak for Adam, but me, I thought maybe it would be fairer to say she didn't recognise me happy, so she didn't realise it might be a factor.

Not that it would have made a difference. Once she decided we were moving, off we went. Again.

"Is it because of me?" Adam asked, after a while.

No, no, don't think that, why would it be? She's always on at me to make friends. Just because I never did before, don't think you're someone special, someone to be run away from. It's the six-month cycle, that's all, her ticking clock. It starts running down the moment she has a key in the lock of the new front door.

I might have said that, some of that, all of it. It was all there to be said, and maybe he wanted to hear it. He'd heard it all before.

But I was bitter, truth was a sour thing in my mouth that day; I said, "I don't know. Maybe it is. Maybe she wants us back the way we were, just the three of us, the story of my life. She says I can have a dog. She says that's

why we're moving, she's found a house where we can keep
a dog."

"You could have a dog where you are. The old lady
wouldn't mind."

"The old lady wouldn't notice. I know that, you know
that. She knows that, and so does Small. It's an excuse.
Or it's a bribe, maybe, a substitute for you. I can't have a
friend, but hey, I can have a dog. Yee-hah."

"Tell you what else you can have," he said suddenly,
"you can have my old bike. Dad's getting me a new one
for my birthday."

I looked at him. "What's that, another kind of bribe?
Make it easy from both sides?"

"No. What I mean is, I'll have a bike, you'll have a bike
you can actually ride. The city's not that big. We don't
have to lose touch. We don't have to lose anything."

That wasn't true, we both knew it, and so did Small.
Moving is always about loss. Whatever you've got that
matters, you can't take it with you when you go. But he
was offering me a lifeline, a way to knot the string behind
my mother's blade. It might have been the first time I'd
ever seen a way to work against her, and someone else had
to show it to me. It might well have been the first time I
ever understood the value of a friend not cut from my own
body, not forced to shape himself within the cavities of my
own thought. Someone who could think a different way
from me, from us; someone who had resources we didn't
share, and was willing to share them with us. It was novel,
it was frightening almost, it gave another axis to the world.
There had been height and breadth already, not me and

Small but us and our mother; now suddenly there was a third dimension, where Adam ran at right angles to us all. Of course I was frightened, how not? He was offering me a leg up, a hand to pull me out; he was showing me vistas and enchantment, and I had thought that Small was all I'd ever need, and he was showing me that I was wrong.

I want to love my brother, I want to love my life. I want a life that I can love. I want to see past my mother, I want to squeeze past my mother, I want to run ahead. I want to run with my friend, I want my brother at my side and running too. I want us all to run together in a world where we all want to do that. I want not to be weird. I want to roll down a hill in the sunshine, laughing, and lie all tangled at the bottom, all three of us, my friend and my brother and me, and not know whose leg that is, or who I'm lying on. And then I want to grow up ...

IV

BEING SMALL

Handsome is as handsome does, and so is Small. What he does gets me into trouble, which is small of him, but that's the thing with brothers. They are, they can be small; they're certainly not heavy. I suppose he's my little brother, any way you want to measure it: born my twin inside me, or else born after me, a couple of years delayed. Born out of me, if you reckon it that way. Younger than me, whichever way you want to reckon it. Two years old at best, a couple of minutes at worst, and the gap between us just keeps on stretching as I grow and move on and he never does. Death is the oil of time, it keeps things moving, rolling along, we'd all be static else; but oil also makes a great preservative.

Born of a virgin — me — and born to die: I could come over all theological, but it's not very useful. God and Small, they're both immanent, they're both allusive, neither one stands up well on their own but they go very well together. The God of Small Things, Small Gods — the parallels are as easy and obvious as the word-games, but ask me what the difference is between them and that too is easy and obvious. Small exists.

You don't believe me? Well, there's the genius in the bottle, I told you about that, but that's the least of him. He's the genius in my life, evil or otherwise; he plays cat's-cradle with my destiny between his chubby and foreshortened fingers. I'm the strong one, the survivor, but it doesn't always feel that way.

Small is as Small does, which is handsome of him. It's always good to know just where you stand. Me, I stand in his shadow, in his tiny shade, it's a thing big brothers have to do. Being there is what matters, and of course I always am.

Small has always, always been the trouble in my life. When we were little, when we were alone together and something got broken or spilled, even where I took the blame it was his awkward hand that had made it happen. I made myself his whipping-boy, because I could; at the same time I made it clear to my mother, to be sure she understood, because there was no point in being a martyr if no one noticed. When she came into our room in the dark of the night and found us with the radio on, the World Service whispering news we had no other access to or opinions that were strangely in opposition to hers, it was always Small who had switched it on. Sometimes I wasn't even listening, sometimes I was sleeping till she woke me. I used to tell her that, every time. She used to smile and say, "I know. He's a bad boy, that Small. It's a wonder that we still put up with him. And yet we do, don't we? He must be worth something, then. Go back to sleep now, both of you, it's a long day tomorrow and the nights are short." That was her slogan, her soundbite, the shout-line that she lived by; we heard it time and time again, and it was nothing to do with the season or the sunrise. She was all signed up for the march of time, onward and upward, do-it-yourself improvement. Every day in every way we had to get better and better, and that required room to grow, the space and freedom of an eternal summer. Nights were short because she insisted on it.

We were boys; for us the night hours could be long. Sometimes, the best times, when she went back to her own room and her own bed, she'd forget to switch off the radio as she went, so we could go on listening. Batteries were the only issue. She rationed us, one new set a month. I could be angry with Small if he listened while I dozed. When we had silent nights, sometimes whole weeks of them if he'd drained too much power too soon, I could be so angry I wouldn't speak to him for days. Being dead, he didn't need much sleep; he must have been terribly bored, in the dark, without me. But I couldn't always keep a hold on his perspective when I lay in the dark myself, wide awake and nothing to listen to.

Nothing except Small, whispering to me. Sometimes that was why I liked the radio. He wanted it to drown the silence, and I wanted it to drown out him. He was my brother and I loved him, but I could still be glad of another voice in my head. He could be really annoying when he tried.

No, I take that back. He never had to try. Not like my

mother, ours, she really worked at it. With Small it was second nature. First nature, maybe, the only one he knew. He was my twin and he died, which was bad; he came out of me to do it, which was worse; and then he didn't have the grace to go away. The dead should leave us alone, us the living. Sometimes I believe that with a fervour that even takes me by surprise.

Small, though, he doesn't believe it at all. At the start, when he'd done with filling my belly, he filled my head and my imagination instead, all the time my mother left me and more besides, so that I had no space for friends or anyone. Then when I showed signs of finding a world, a life apart from him, he did his best to trash it. He made me weird, so that all those friends-in-embryo decided that they had no time for me.

And when I found one friend despite his best endeavours, one friend and then slowly, cautiously more than one, when I started reaching, stretching beyond the bottle, swimming outside the glass — well, that's when he really got mean.

Short, pale and anything but handsome, even without his jar, Small makes a great pickled gooseberry.

V

CARBON DATING

I want my voice to break. *I want my heart to break. I want to be adopted. I want to learn that I was adopted. I want to go swimming, I want to go scrumping, I want to go slippery and wet and pinching apples. I want someone to pinch me. I want to sleep with someone older, someone a lot older, I want to be in all the tabloids. I want to be left alone. I want to know that I'm wanted...*

I never wanted to be sixteen, neither of us did, but it happens. It does happen. We had our party on the move, halfway between houses, all packed up at one and barely started unpacking at the next. There seemed to be an ever-increasing heap of boxes, bags, plants in pots, bits of furniture and bicycles in bits. Every time we moved Mum borrowed a bigger van, and still we had to make more trips back and forth, up and down more stairs. We lived our lives in attics, in servants' rooms and loft conversions, gazing out through dormer windows at rain on slant slate rooftops. Every year it became harder to fit in. The luggage of our lives constricted us, and I banged my head on rafters with a frequency that was close to pathological.

Actually, be fair. It was most of it my luggage. One hoarder, among the three of us; I never could bear to let anything go.

I didn't want to let my brother go, but I could feel its happening, or the threat of it, building.

. . .

Sixteen was too big, was the trouble. All those accumulated years, years of accumulation, they were taking me out of his reach. He used to wind his little arms and legs around me, but I was filling out so much he could barely snatch a hold; long gone, his stranglehold.

I was growing into an imitation freedom, a first adolescent glimpse of big-sky thinking, and I really didn't like it. Given my choice, I'd have gone back. Not far, not all the way: back to twelve, perhaps, back to a bad bike and a first friend and a fumbling after some kind of balance. Good days. I could have stayed that way for ever, swaying between brother and mother and Adam, long days out and long nights in and talking, talking all the time.

I wasn't given my choice, of course. No one ever is. No one except Small, who got to stay exactly as he was and always had been, me in a frozen moment long ago. We might still be identical, but it was getting harder and harder to see us together, so who knew if they could tell us apart?

. . .

This latest move, this party-on-the-move wasn't taking us anywhere new. There was nowhere new in the city, we'd moved so often and lived everywhere: only places to be re-discovered, histories to be reinstated, *this is where we came to fly your kite that Christmas and the bad wind took it away* and *that used to be the butcher, do you remember him, a foul-tempered man who hated kids and wouldn't have you in the shop?* I thought I'd been a happy child, more or less, but it seemed like all the memories were bad, even if they were told these days with a smile. The good stuff leaches away, I guess, or it just doesn't have anything to cling with. Fear and ugliness and disappointment, those are velcro.

So we were coming back to where we'd been ten years ago, a shady lane of pre-war semis that overlooked a park, to the east of the city and up. I felt like a nomad child on a long, long loop, something more than seasonal, follow-ing a call that only my mother heard. Except that I was sixteen and didn't feel like any kind of child any more, and it wasn't long now that I would have to go on follow-ing my mother. I could spare her this at least, some part of one more birthday.

Between one load and the next, then, we parked the hire-van on the verge of a little wood at the lane's end, where I used to lose myself in beetle-hunts and playing hide-and-seek with Small. We sat in the empty back of the van with the doors wide and our legs dangling, and we drank apple-juice because cider would be irresponsible,

she said, with more driving yet to do. I said I didn't like
cider anyway, and she said that wouldn't have stopped her
getting it in, and I said I knew that so I was glad she'd had
some other reason not to do it. She asked if I was saying
she was selfish, and I said yes, of course I was. All her
life probably, all my life for sure, I said, had been shaped
to her own desires. My life and Small's death, I said, all
this long time we'd spent just doing what pleased her.
She asked what it was that we wanted instead, what we
would have done differently; I said I couldn't tell her, we
didn't know, we'd never had the chance to find out. She
said that was a cop-out and I said no, we were the way she
had made us, we'd been cut to fit and I just had to live
with that, Small just had to deal with it, just for a while
longer.

   She went quiet at that, and I thought perhaps we were
going to have an all-out row. It was still quite a recent
discovery, that we could do that and go on living together
as we did, half in each other's pockets and half entirely independent, off and away. I had no temper, I didn't fight, it
was Small who was vicious and tantrum-prone; anger only
made me silent, perhaps in reaction to him. Sometimes,
when you're twins, there's an imperative to asymmetry, to
unmatch, just to be sure that you each of you exist. With
Small it was never such a problem, but even so I used to
indulge the impulse consciously sometimes, and I think
more often unaware.

   My mother used to say I sulked, but that was a mis-
understanding, so it had to be deliberate. For myself I
just thought that I got clagged up, choked off with fury,

nowhere to go but inward. That it was possible to fight without being angry had been a revelation, and remained a development that I think we were both watching with interest. Far from stirring up any anger inside me — and how could it be fresh in any case, after so long a time? Nothing but dregs and ashes at best, not worth the kindling — her utter self-absorption was a touchstone, recognition, safe home again. Still, I was quite willing to fight about it if she wanted to.

She only went quiet for a while, though, and then said, "Do you want your presents now?"

"Well, yeah, if you've got 'em. I'm seeing Adam later. I just thought they'd be all scrambled up in the boxes and you wouldn't find 'em for weeks." If she found them at all, if she'd bought them at all, if she'd given our birthday any thought at all except to fix it as a good day for a move.

"Don't be silly, sunbeam. Presents matter." They mattered to her, that much I did know. She was always good at giving things away. And I was still half a kid, I could still be full-on child when I tried, they could matter very much to me also; but because I was still half a kid, I was trying very much to pretend that they did not. "I wouldn't let them get mixed up with the move. They're in the footwell, that carrier bag you were folding your legs around. I did tell you not to kick it."

"Oh. Okay. Thanks." That meant no big boxes: no skateboard, no laptop, nothing that I knew I really wanted. No matter. When did we ever get what we really wanted? Maybe they were all for Small. More likely they were just what she really wanted to give us. "I'll fetch them, shall I?"

"No, you stay. I'll go." And she went, crawling back through the van's body and stretching over the passenger seat, fumbling out a carrier-bag and dragging it into the light, puffing audibly as she settled again beside me.

"Wouldn't it have been easier to walk round, open the door, lean in?"

"Yes, of course. When did I ever do anything the easy way? I had you, remember, the two of you. And chose to bring you up on my own and full-time, no man, no dumping either of you on grandparents or schools. I only like things difficult."

I said that was probably just as well in the circumstances, but didn't spell them out. I had my little history of troubles and a certainty of more to come, some she knew about and some she didn't. No doubt the same was true of her, that there were secret struggles, private shames she hadn't shared with me. I really didn't want to know it all. Sometimes I wondered if she had an undeclared reason to keep us moving on, but never far. Perhaps she was afraid that something, someone might be gaining on us; perhaps she was half-hoping to be caught. I never asked, for fear she might tell me.

"I didn't make such a bad job of you, either," she said, eyeing me up and down. "All things considered. Open your presents. And your brother's, his as well. Do you want them one by one, or all together?"

"I want to lay them out, see who gets what."

"Child. Where did you get that competitive instinct? Not from me. Nor from your father, as far as I could ever tell. He was a man of great disinterest."

"It's not competition, it's comparison — and I do it on Small's behalf. There's usually more for me."

"Never mind the quantity, feel the wit."

It was true that his presents tended to be better, either because she tried harder or else because she didn't try so hard. It didn't matter. I got to play with them all, as he did, share and share alike. Small and I, we really did have no secrets from each other and nothing private to ourselves; which only made it all the more important that our presents were separately wrapped and labelled, his and mine.

No big boxes, but the carrier bag was half the size of Santa's sack, if not so fatly stuffed. I drew out all the contents and arranged them in two piles; as usual, mine was larger and his felt more expensive. I quickly got a pattern running: one from my pile, one from his, one from mine again and then a drink, a word with Mum, repeat. That way I could spread out the disproportion, not to be left with half a heap for me and no further interest for him.

There were books, of course, there were always books. Books were half the furniture of my life. Second-hand furniture, for the most part. There was Greek and astronomy for me, the poetry of Robert Lowell and Gerard Manley Hopkins, all of last year's Whitbread winners — those bought new in paperback, to keep me au fait with contemporary tastes, she said — and a random selection of charity-shop crime. Those last would be deliberately hit-and-miss, all part of her campaign to teach me that it was good to pass things on, okay to throw them away. So far, the lesson wasn't taking. Even the bad books I hung on to,

along with all my childhood reading, all my elementary
textbooks, everything.

For Small there was just the one book, as he'd never
learned to read. I used to enjoy reading to him, but my
mother found it hard going to persuade me now, though
she did persist.

Just the one book, then, but a fat one. "*Le Comte de
Monte-Cristo*?" I murmured, gazing at her, as neutral as I
could manage.

"Your accent needs work," she said crisply. "I can listen
in sometimes, to correct you."

"Every time, then, or I don't start."

"I can't promise that, with shiftwork. You know I can't."

"That's okay, I'll read in shifts."

She frowned at me, and sighed, and said, "Your poor
brother. I'll try, Michael. Open something else."

Summer clothes for me, jeans and T-shirts in bright
mother-colours, with ostentatious logos that weren't quite
right, weren't at all what they were hoping to be mistaken
for. For Small something better, a pocket electronic chess
game. It looked twenty years old and maybe older, but the
batteries were fresh and all the pieces were there. Who
cared if the logo was missing and the plastic cover had a
crack in it, the hinge was held together with gaffer tape
and the edges were worn shiny? Not us.

"It's got an 'undefeated' level," my mother pointed out,
like a challenge.

"So've I."

"I know. That's why Small needs to practise."

It was true, my little brother never had beaten me

yet. I made the ritual protest, "That's just an excuse, to give him the best presents." She said, "Of course it is, I don't need telling that," and I went on cheerfully unwrapping, with the odd gloating glance back at the ChessLord.

That was prime, the prince of presents, but the last of mine had its own happy talent. It was light, it lay in the palm of my hand, it gave a little metallic jingle as I tossed it palm to palm. We don't play guessing-games, my mother and I, so I said, "It's the key."

"Open it and see," she suggested, smiling with a hint of smug.

So I opened it, and of course it was the key to our new lodgings. I had a collection that had been growing for six or seven years now. My mother always had one cut for me, so I saw no need to give it to our landlord as we left. Each one came with its own key-ring and fob, as a treat and a distinguishing feature; I could remember which key belonged to which house, all the baker's dozen of them with all their hoarded, sordid histories.

A couple of the fobs had my initials on, carved in wood or etched in steel. Others were pretty things, polished stone or silver plaitwork. One wasn't a fob at all, it was a beaded leather string for wearing round my neck. That had given me the necklace habit; when I'd had to take it off, next time we moved, Adam replaced it with a thick gold chain that hung heavy on the nape of my neck, rippled over my collar-bones and pressed into the point of my throat when I lay back. There'd been trouble over that, my mother thought it was too expensive to accept.

I might have told her that it had cost him nothing, that he'd stolen it for me, but I was fourteen and not actually stupid. I told her it had been a gift to him but he had enough already, too many to choose from; he was thinning out his dressing-room, I said, passing on what he didn't need, she had to approve of that. She grunted, and let me keep it. I made him pinch another, made him wear it visibly to lend verisimilitude.

I was wearing the chain now, I wore it always: in bed, in the shower, everywhere. I slipped my thumb beneath to pull it tight and slid a finger over the smooth suppleness of its links, as I grinned at the finger-sized Homer Simpson in my hand, with the key-ring hanging from his grasp.

"Throw it away," my mother said.

"Do what?"

"Throw it away. Oh, no, you can't do that, can you? Here ..."

And she did, she just picked it up and tossed it, a casual five or six metres into the shadow and the undergrowth of the wood. I saw where it fell, but only dimly.

"Mum ...!"

"Now whistle."

"Do what?"

"Whistle. You can do that, I know. I endured the months you spent learning."

Well, I'd had to learn. I was a boy, I had a friend, whistling was a necessary accomplishment. More than that, I'd had a dog, too briefly.

I blew the two-note call I used to use for Max, but barely on a breath.

"Perhaps a little louder?"

I did it again, shrill and hard; in answer, from the undergrowth, came Homer's trademark "D'oh!"

When I could manage it, when I'd stopped choking on the giggles, I did it again. And then again, and eventually she said, "Actually it's meant to help you find it when it's lost, it isn't a John Cage duet for one voice and a transponder. I'm bored with this. Go fetch."

I went to find and fetch it, whistling all the way; and more than Homer answered me. There was a sudden rush-and-skitter, all the familiar sounds of an eager and awkward body charging blindly. I had a moment to wonder if I was going to grieve again, cry again, lose my heart and hope again, before a mess of black came hurtling out between the trees and plunged at me, all eyes and fur and tangled limbs and happy mouth and heavy.

Heavy enough that I sat down on the thin grass there and had young dog in my lap and all over me, his paws on my shoulders, his tongue in my mouth. I hugged him, because what else could I do? And told him he was fast, he was forward, we hadn't been introduced and I never snogged on a first date. My mother's snort at my back might have meant anything; I didn't care. By now I was on my back and he was play-growling with his teeth oh so gently around my wrist while his tail thrashed widely, wildly as we wrestled.

Distantly I heard voices with an anxious edge to them, calling a name he paid no attention to. Not a birthday present, then: neither a sneaky one from Mum nor a gift from any passing god, a stray dog needing shelter. Not a gift to keep. Okay, I could live with that, without this. I'd been doing it for months.

"Nigel! Nigel, you futile fucking creature, where the shit have you got to this time ...?"

They came out suddenly from the shadows beneath the trees, two men. Nigel and I spared them a glance apiece and then decided to go on romping, while the same voice said, "Oh, whoops. Sorry about the language. And the dog."

"Ill-trained, the pair of them," the other man said. "They're not mine, I'm just walking them for a friend. Shouldn't have let that one off the lead, really. It's not that he doesn't come when he's called — he just comes when anyone calls, whoever they are. Or whistles."

"We noticed," my mother said, a little dryly. "Michael, perhaps you'd better hang on to his collar, if he's liable to go shooting off again."

The dog wasn't going anywhere, he was having far too much fun. He'd squirmed out of my grasp and was playing with the wrapping-paper now, pouncing stiff-legged into the pile of it and grabbing mouthfuls, shaking them and scattering them like rats.

"Oh, God. Nigel ...!" One of the men grabbed him then, while the other snatched at the mangled paper before the wind could take it. I stood up to help, saw that I wasn't needed and went to talk to the dog again. Even on the lead he was happy, bouncing, jumping up as if all the soul of him were in his teeth and his tongue and that was strong enough to lift him as high as he wanted to go.

It was the older man who had control of Nigel. The

other might be half his age, early twenties, blond and pretty and knowing it, groomed for it. He gathered up armsful of paper and took them back to my mother, saying, "Somebody's birthday?"

"The twins," my mother said, nodding in my direction. "They're sixteen."

"Nice. Set the controls for the heart of the sun. But I'm afraid we've pooped your party." His voice was light and lemony, tart enough to shiver me.

"Not to worry. We were just having a break to do their presents, but we should get back to work anyway. There's another vanload to shift yet, and I'd like to be in before dark. Find that key, Michael, and we'll get on. If you've finished winding up the dog."

Obviously, I hadn't. The guy on the other end of the lead twitched an eyebrow at me and said, "Aren't you missing someone? Twins, she said."

"My brother died," I said quickly, before my mother could, "but he still gets his presents." Sometimes she could sound quite mad, when she talked about Small. I could say the exact same things and just sound haunted.

"Ah. I'm sorry. Of course he does, that would be important."

His friend was checking over the heap of presents as he spoke, where they were piled just inside the van's door. "Oh, hey — you play chess?"

"Sure." *We both do, but I'm better* — it was on the tip of my tongue, and for a wonder that's where it stayed, even while my mother waited to hear it.

"Fancy a game sometime, just come by the house.

Number thirty-nine, up the lane there, and say you're a chessmaster. You'll be welcome."

"I'm not —"

But I was overridden by my mother's saying, "Number thirty-nine? We're almost neighbours, then. Michael and I are Mrs Alleyn's new lodgers, along at forty-seven."

"That right? Welcome to the neighbourhood. We don't know the neighbours; we don't actually live here, see. Just come by to walk the dog and be useful. But definitely, come round and play chess. Any time. Come tonight, and we can introduce you."

"Can't," I said, not too sorry. I don't like being rushed. "I'm out with a friend tonight."

"Of course you are, you're sixteen. Crash and burn. Well, come soon, then."

"He will," my mother promised for me, she who loves to rush things. "Who should he ask for?"

"Doesn't matter, really. Chess is the password. But — oh. You mean, who are we, that you should trust your boy to us? Sorry. Again. I'm Kit, and that's Peter," his more solid friend, dark and quiet, like an anchor. "The dog's Nigel, but you know that already."

My mother introduced herself and me, and said that my brother was called Small; and then of course she said, "And if the dog needs a regular walker, I think Michael would be happy to help." So swift, so keen she was to give me all away.

"Oh, cool. A chess-playing dogwalker. Couldn't be better. Peter, can we adopt him?"

"Only for the duration. And with his mother's consent. Michael, never mind Kit; if you want to come by, please do. Not only Nigel will be pleased to see you, though I think we can promise that," as the dog chewed rapturously at my hand again. "Look for the Merc in the drive and you'll know I'm there, if you're shy to call on strangers. Kit drives a silver Mini, if you want to avoid him. Come on now, you two. Heel," and it wasn't clear if he was talking to Nigel or Kit, but neither one of them paid him any attention as they left. Nigel strained back towards me for a fickle little moment, then leaped ahead, trying to drag Peter after; Kit bestowed a last sunny smile on the pair of us like a blessing, and sauntered off in their wake.

"All right, son?"

"Yes, of course." I wasn't so sure about the chess; there was a security in only ever playing Small, and always winning. But the men had piqued more than my curiosity, and Nigel had stolen my heart.

"Good. Extra birthday present, then. Thank your pushy mother who levered you into it, and call by sometime in the week. That kind of invitation has a use-by date. Especially if you want to be official dogwalker, you've got to look keen and reliable. Go tomorrow, while we're unpacking; the break will do you good. So will having more friends than one. You spend too much time with Adam."

She built too swiftly, and too high. I saw no signs of budding friendship here, small hopes of it. It was the dog I wanted, and I'd play chess as the price, even with grown-ups. I was sixteen; I didn't make friends with grown-ups. I didn't make friends with anyone but Adam. But, "I know that, Mum. At least, I know you think that. I'm not stupid."

She said nothing, she only whistled sharply and unexpectedly, and Homer said "D'oh!" in the long grass.

. . .

We'd fixed to meet at his house, and when I got there — for which read, when my mother at last let me go — I found Adam enmeshed with his sister and his sister's friends, a perfumed stew of teenage girls hugging cushions and watching television. Even those who'd never met me knew who I was, and what I was to them, which was a freak. They eyed me askance and pretty much silently, holding back whatever whispers and shrieks my appearance might provoke. The first time I'd been introduced to Charlotte and her cohorts, I'd betrayed myself twice over: first by answering all the questions on *The Weakest Link*, which made me a geek if not a nerd, and then by talking about Small. Adam had patted me on the shoulder like a kindly uncle giving the brash young idiot nephew a hint, *shut up now*, and then he'd taken me away and tried to explain about girls.

The lesson really hadn't taken, or else my position was irrecoverable. I was the creepy genius kid who didn't want to win quiz shows, who had a ghostly twin that I still talked to, for God's sake, as if he was really there, and how weird is that? And I didn't go to school and I didn't have any friends except Adam, and he was pretty weird himself by their lights. Like my mother, they thought we spent far too much time together. Every now and then Charlotte tried to save him from himself, which meant from me, but she wasn't cut out for missionary work; she lacked patience, and in the end she lacked commitment. Only her brother, after all, and boys were strange by nature. There was probably no point trying to meddle.

So she cut our hair for us whenever we'd let her, but mostly we were left alone, in a very literal sense. Which was of course what we wanted, if no one else did. Small didn't like it at all. He could be mean that way, possessive. I understood him perfectly. I had the best of both worlds and he had the other thing; I was all the world he had and he wanted to keep it to himself. Of course he did, how not? If I'm no angel, he's no saint.

And this was our birthday, and I was surprised, almost shocked when he let me go. It had been harder to get away from our mother, with her ready excuses: so many boxes to shift and empty, new quarters to settle into, no night this for gadding about with my mate when I could do that any time and she needed my strong arms and my long reach. I suggested fetching Adam over, for extra arms and extra reach, but she didn't buy it. Double trouble, she said, which was fair enough. He'd helped us move once before, and it had taken all day. Twice the boys meant half the work, she said, and I couldn't argue. That had been half the plan. So I worked twice as hard instead, and wouldn't stay for supper; and Adam's family of course had eaten before I got there, so he and I were entirely out of kilter with each other.

"Cheese sandwich?" he suggested, in that particular tone of voice that's only waiting to be refused.

"Kebab," I said positively. "And chips."

"Oh. Only, I thought we'd stay in ... "

"You thought wrong. Me too, though, if that's any consolation: I was reckoning to stay in. I just have to eat, is all. Come on, let's go frighten the natives."

Two boys don't make a gang but we did our best sometimes, catching a mood between us and responding to it, lifting each other by the bootlaces, greater far than the sum of our parts.

We swaggered and whooped, we made ourselves large and loud and got in people's way, we stopped the traffic and left a chorus of blaring horns in our wake. Adam bought a quarter-bottle of vodka from a friendly corner-shop, I bought a pint of milk; I drank half the milk with my kebab and then we mixed the vodka in and shared it, sip and sip. It's a boy thing.

Then we did the Thursday late-night window-shopping thing, the local version of the *passeggiare*, strutting our best stuff under the eyes of half the city's teens. Spending money wasn't quite the point, the chain-stores generally closed at eight and we just carried on. The food-courts stayed open, though, and so did some of the boutiques that clustered round them. So it was that we could suddenly snatch a whim out of nowhere and indulge it, diving into a cheap little jeweller all tanked up as we were and requesting, demanding this week's special offer.

"Oh, do me a favour, lads! I'm closing in five minutes."

"It's in your window. Two for the price of one, it says. Him and me."

"I know what it says in the window, and I can count, but—"

"It's false advertising if you don't do it. We'll complain. Highest authorities in the land."

"You terrify me. But there's only me in the shop, and I can't leave the till, so—"

"So we'll wait. You lock up, and do us after."

"Can't you just come back tomorrow? The offer's good till Saturday."

"It won't be his birthday tomorrow, will it?"

"Oh, for God's sake. All right. Show us your money then choose what you want, that case there, while I cash up. Don't touch anything else, I've got CCTV."

"Oh, hey, we're not thieves!"

That from Adam, who was wearing the self-same chain that I was and had paid for neither one of them, who could be as light-fingered as he could be heavy-handed when he chose. But we were being good tonight, we were being grand, it was my birthday and there's actually more fun in spending money than there is in getting away with not. Besides which, he was paying, and who knew where the cash had come from ... ?

We stooped over the display case, heads together, each of us shy to choose and waiting for the other; and when he did, of course we had to argue, jeer and elbow and start again. By the time the guy was ready for us, though, so were we ready for him.

"We'll have a pair of those, please, and a pair of those."

"Fair enough. Who gets which?"

"One of each," I said, "for each of us." Wasn't it obvious? "The ring in the left ear, the stud in the right."

"No," Adam said, "the other way round."

I glared at him, drew breath to fight — then lost it, giggled, said, "Well, they're your ears. But that's how I want mine. Either way, your mother's going to slay you."

"Is not. It'll be you that she slays. You're a bad influence, you."

Which was more or less what my own mother felt about him, except that she wouldn't care about piercings. She was probably surprised I'd waited this long, probably a little disappointed; by now she likely thought I should be hiding tattoos. Alas for her peace of mind, all my secrets were much more easily disguised.

. . .

Ten minutes later we were gazing at each other with numb and glittering ears, reeking of antisepsis and not at all listening to the aftercare instructions; and against my tentative grin Adam said, "Hell, who needs a twin? This is like looking in a mirror," and he might as well have been handing out sober-pills, a cold shower, a sudden brutal shock.

He was right, of course. Same hair, same neck-chain, piercings reversed so that it really was like looking in a mirror, and there was something wildly strange in that because it was always Small I saw when I looked at myself, we'd always been identical no matter how I changed. And now suddenly we weren't, I'd done something he couldn't, and matched up with someone else — and on my birthday too, his birthday, ours.

I lost all my dizzy happy feelings in a moment, and walked out quiet and steady and ashamed.

Adam caught up, caught on, said, "You okay?" in that voice that says *I already know you're not.*

"Not really. Sorry. It was a good idea."

"You just shouldn't have gone along with it, you mean."

"Something like that."

"Bit late now. Will you be in trouble?"

"Probably."

"I thought your mum was cool."

"Not with her."

"Oh. Right." He always went silent, sooner than talk about Small. Suited me fine, as a rule and specifically just then.

"It's been a good evening, Adam. Thanks."

"It's not over yet. Night's young, you're not. Come on back, we'll raid the drinks cupboard and watch a movie. Stay over, your mum won't mind."

She never had; but, "No, there's too much to do. I need to get back," and not for my mother's sake. I might be growing apart from Small, but this was a bad day to be showing it.

· · ·

We had a subdued walk back to Adam's, no clowning and not much talk. I felt a long way away from him, for all that we were rubbing shoulders. He tried again to draw me into the house, "just for a coffee," but I shook my head, took my bike and left him.

Pedalled slowly towards the new house, uphill all the way, my mood as dark and heavy as the sky above the streetlights.

Not so many lights in the lane, and I wasn't too sure of the house, to spot it at speed, at night — or that's the excuse I offered myself, as I dismounted and pushed the bike along the pavement. It didn't sound convincing, even to me. Truth was, I was dawdling, putting off the moment, suddenly reluctant to face what I'd come back looking for. My mother, the new house, a new dispensation — I couldn't have stayed with Adam tonight, but nor did I want to deal with what lay waiting for me here.

The sound of scrabbling claws and panting on the road behind me might have been a message from on high, if I believed in deities in or out of the machine; the voice that hailed me had a more earthy message of its own.

"Sweet sixteen. What are you doing, what are you *thinking*, coming home at this hour? It's not eleven o'clock yet. What are you, a rebel with a curfew?"

It was Kit, of course, coming out of the park with Nigel pulling at his lead and desperate to reach me. I might have been cynical, guessing that Nigel pulled desperately at his lead whether anyone or no one was ahead; I decided to be flattered. The bike went up against a wall, I went down on my knees, Nigel slammed into me and we did the boy-and-dog romping thing again, only a little constrained by having Kit stand over us and criticise.

" ... You know, I only brought him out for a last pee before bedtime. Now you're getting him all wound up again ... Oh, look, french kissing on your birthday is a treat, but — well, I've smelled his breath, so if I were you I'd be holding yours. And talking of birthday kisses, you didn't answer my question."

"I know," I grunted, my face in Nigel's neck while he wriggled all over me.

"So? You're supposed to come creeping home with the dawn, all drunk and achy and trying to tiptoe upstairs so your mother won't hear. Have you got an excuse, or are you just too good to live?"

"Not that."

"Have a row with your friend?"

"No. Not really. Just — oh, I don't know. I did something I maybe shouldn't, and I think there's going to be trouble."

"What, with your mother? I thought she seemed quite laid-back."

"Not with her. My brother."

A little pause, then, "You've got another brother?"

"No. Just my twin."

"Sorry, I thought he was dead ...?"

"He is. That doesn't stop him having opinions."

"Oh. O-kay. Interesting. You want to talk about it? You'd better come in anyway, it's far too early to go home. And you can play tug-of-war with Nigel, he won't settle now without and you're the one who got him so excited,

so you're the one can have his shoulder wrenched out of
joint. He may look skinny, but he's got a wicked pull on
him. And then you can meet Quin; he won't be sleeping."

"Uh, who's Quin?"

"Quin's the boss. Master of the house. He's the reason
we all keep coming round. Come on, sixteen. I'm not
letting you home in this condition."

"My name's Michael."

"Sweet."

. . .

He wouldn't even let me take the bike home, he said
he didn't trust me to come back. I left it chained to a
telegraph pole and followed obediently where he and
Nigel led me.

Like Mrs Alleyn's up the lane, number thirty-nine was
a big semi-detached house set back behind a small front
garden steeply banked. There was a garden gate with a
stepped path climbing to a tiled porch, the front door, a
big windowed bay. Mum and I didn't get to use the front
door, and neither apparently did Nigel; he towed Kit up
the drive beside the garden, where three cars were parked
nose-to-tail. No Merc, no Peter. Kit's silver Mini was the
middle of the three. He'd said they didn't live here, but
I wondered if he'd be staying the night. I was wondering
a lot about this household, and determined not to ask, if
only because I thought he was waiting for the questions.

Curtains masked the front windows but soft light
was leaking out at the margins, carried on a thin wash

of music. The third car, a big old Volvo estate, squeezed us close to the side of the house. Our new lodgings had a separate door for us in this wall, opening onto a staircase that took us straight up to the mini-flat among the gables. Not so here; Nigel dragged us around to the back, to a flat-roofed recent offshoot with enough glass in the walls that they might have called it a conservatory when it went up. Now it was part garage, part garden shed, mostly dog-room. Here was water, that Nigel thrust his face into and splashed; here were empty food-bowls, that he investigated in a spirit of hopeless optimism; here were toys that he fetched to drop at our feet, and a basket-bed that he ignored entirely.

Tug-of-war was the game of choice, to be played with an old rope bound into two loops, each end wet and chewed to fraying. My arms and shoulders were aching already, at this back end of a day spent hauling boxes down stairs and into van, out of van and up; so at first I just hung on two-handed, leaning back against the frantic jerking heaves that utilised every last bone and muscle Nigel had, from gripping teeth to counterweighting tail. There's a pleasure, though, in working to exhaustion, and in the growing pains next day. Once I was sure I could hold him, I took him on one arm at a time, testing biceps and deltoid, lifting till he was almost hanging, front paws pedalling the air. He was wild for it, locked jaw and glittering eyes, a menacing growl quite denied by his rotary tail. Me, too. I couldn't see my eyes, but I was doing my equivalent of the threatening growl: "Come on then, if you think you're hard enough; is that all you've got, you wuss...?" in a constant undertone, and if I'd had a tail I would surely have been threshing it.

My right arm was done and my left was doing nicely by the time Kit came back. He'd gone on into the house murmuring something about coffee, which wasn't what he'd offered in the street outside; and he'd been gone a while, and his hands were empty, and he said, "That's better. It's a new game, or else it's a psychological theory I've just come up with, based on the scissors-paper-stone model: boy tames wolf, wolf exhausts master, master humiliates boy. Where wolf is the purely animal, master is the purely intellectual and boy is something borderline between, all shaken up and waiting to settle. Nigel, go to bed. Michael, come through; Quin's ready for you now."

To my surprise and perhaps a little to his own, Nigel did go to bed: a little slinky, a little downcast, tail low and sidelong glances as though this were a punishment undeserved. Kit reached into a bag on a shelf, found a biscuit the size of a small bone and tossed it casually underhand. Nigel took it on the fly and in the manner it was meant, as ritual compensation for a ritual complaint. He curled up in his basket, crunching woefully; Kit turned out the light and beckoned me through.

This was the back door proper, opening into a scullery — washing-machine, dryer, big chest freezer that looked old in itself but newly come, not fully fitted in yet, standing proud of the wall and slightly at an angle, inconvenient in its size and placement both — and then the kitchen. I was an expert on kitchens, I'd seen and used so many, trying first to encourage and then to teach my mother to cook for me. This one was not big enough for the house. What must always have been too cramped for comfort had become breathless and busy, cupboards everywhere and every surface cluttered. It was scrupulously clean, which might have been surprising and somehow was not; but the toaster and food processor and mixer and blender and juicer and breadmaker and coffeemaker and knifeblock and breadboard and so on left precious little room for cooking.

No matter. There was a smell of coffee in the air; there was an open doorway and a passage on, and Kit was there and looking back to find me. I hurried forward, and found myself suddenly walled in with books. They were floor-to-ceiling, on either side of the passage and in the hall beyond, running upstairs and out of sight.

"Quin reads a lot," Kit said. "Used to, at least. He gets tired now. The house is built of books, but we're going to have to move these, they're in the way. Just the thought of it makes me tired. Strong young volunteers welcome. I'll let you know."

And then he opened another door, that must lead into the front room; and he went inside, and actually I was feeling unnerved and would rather have stayed out there and looked at books, but he didn't give me the chance.

"Quin, here's Michael. Loves dogs, loves to read. The rest he can tell you himself."

• • •

So I walked in; and if I thought it was shadowy in the passage outside, under the watchful weight of all those books — well, I was wrong, that's all. You need light, to make shadows. Quin had plenty of lights, dim little lights all around him, and all they did was make shadow. That was what they were for. The longer I knew him, the more truth I found in that, and the less comfort.

That first night I edged in, not looking for comfort, not sure what I was looking for, or what I ought to find; and found myself confronted, jarred by answers to several of the questions I hadn't asked, all at once and unexpectedly.

This again was lined with books, this room. Heavy sun-struck curtains made another wall, just as dark, that followed the curve of the bay; but there was a standard lamp dressed in an old shade, there were desk-lamps and table-lamps, plenty light enough to say how pleasant it must have been to sit in here and read, in the days when he could do that without thinking.

Actually Quin never did anything without thinking, but I didn't know that yet. All I knew was that I was looking into a world well lost, a place displaced from its purpose. The desk and sofa and easy chairs were all pushed back to the sides of the room, hard against the bookcases, all to make space for a bed. A high bed, a hospital bed, tubular metal frame designed for lifting and lowering and moving around on polished hygienic surfaces, not at all designed to have its castors sunk into an ageing, fading Chinese rug.

"Michael. Come and sit, be welcome. Kit, he needs a drink."

In the bed was a man, was undoubtedly Quin, and no more was he designed for this. His bed had been transposed, imported; he'd been shrunk to fit. Even half-sitting as he was, with the mattress raised at an angle and pillows banked behind him, he still had to look up to see me, who would never be as tall as he was. As he used to be. He'd had his height and lost it, that was written into him, in the length of the legs that wouldn't hold him up. And his weight had gone too, leaving his hands like wicker where they jutted from the sleeves of his silk kimono and his face ill-fitted to his skull or his age or his history. His hair was salt-and-pepper, white and grey and brown sifted together in an unexpected crew-cut, the last least vigour left to him. His eyes were wide and dark, and I wondered what drugs he was on, what could keep a man so tired and so alert. Fear could do that, and desire could do it, and together they were sovereign but you can't get those on prescription.

"Already on it." Kit was busy at the desk in the window, where a tray stood awkwardly balanced on books and sheaves of paper. His hands moved between bottles and a cafetière, and I might just have stood and watched him work; or there were more books here and I might have drifted over to the wall to look at them, except that I couldn't manage that degree of ease, or else of disobedience. *Come and sit,* he had said. He might have lost height and breadth, but he still had all the depth he needed. Not in his eyes, they were flat and shimmered only on the surface; not in his voice, which was reedy and hollowed out, sounding like a tracing of what it must have been, another intractable measurement of loss. Everything he had seemed stubbornly to define what he had been, how far he'd fallen and was falling still.

That should have been a weakness, a statement of defeat, and it was not. I didn't know where it lay, the sense of strength abiding. I felt it, though, and responded in the simplest way, like a dog to a whistle, blindly trusting. Except that I wasn't blind and I didn't trust, excepting only that. The prince of darkness is a gentleman; Lucifer must still have had an angel's air about him as he fell. He never could disguise or deny what he was made of, the very stuff of heaven. I would tread warily here, and commit myself to nothing.

Except that coming to the bedside, sitting on the upright chair provided — high to match the bed, so that my feet were just a fraction off the floor, which felt appropriate — even so little obedience was a commitment, of a sort. Here I sat; I could do no other. For now.

Closer, I could see how the skin around his eyes should have been creased and shadowed, how all his face should have held his age in its folds but had lost it, only the shallowest of pale lines left like parch marks in his tan. Sickness was working on him as botox does, drawing his skin tight and smoothing out all his wrinkles. Perhaps he should market it, blood in a bottle, a liquid facelift...

Except that this close, that wasn't a tan, it was jaundice that coloured him so highly; and that drug-sheen lay

on his eyes like an oil slick, so bright and so unhealthy;
and no, no one could ever want to buy into this.

"My new neighbour, then. Mrs Alleyn may have got it
right for once. Kit says you like dogs, and you play chess."

"He does. Kit also says, drink this," and was standing
at my elbow with a steaming mug of coffee. Black, and
presumably unsweetened, but he wasn't offering me cream
or sugar. I took it, stricken shy again, and he said, "Drink
it quickly, it's not that hot."

Which seemed an odd thing to say, and unlikely to be
true, freshly made and freshly poured. I took a wary sip,
ready to pretend but not to burn my tongue — and almost
choked on the simple surprise of it, warm and dense and
sweet, barely coffee at all.

"What is it?"

"Café trèche," he said; and then perhaps heard his
own smugness and tried to correct it, because he went on,
"Quin taught us."

"I taught them all," dryly, from the bed. "All they
know, which is not much more than what you hold in
your hands there, but at least that lesson stuck."

"What's in it?" I asked, taking another swallow, bolder
now.

"Brandies," Kit said. "Poire William and slivovitz, tonight. Next time it might be apricot and peach, anything
fruity."

"It's wonderful, thank you."

"You're welcome." He'd been busy while he spoke,
setting up a chessboard on a bed-tray that he laid now

across the patient's knees. I wanted to say no, I wasn't ready, I wasn't even willing, I hadn't been asked; but long and fragile fingers were reaching already, not to move yet, just to touch, and those tender fluttery gestures broke whatever will was in me to resist him.

"You can have white," Quin said, and indeed the board stood that way round, Kit had just assumed it. "Do you need a handicap on top? I could spot you a knight or a rook, if it makes for a better game."

"I don't need a handicap," I said quietly. "Do you?"

He quirked an eyebrow. "Well, then. Let's find out."

. . .

I thought that this would be a getting-to-know-you game, a social occasion, that we would talk as we played. That he would ask me questions. That was all my experience of an adult world, that grown-ups asked me questions. Sometimes, in self-defence, I'd refer them to my brother. "You'd better ask Small about that, I wouldn't know," or sometimes, "He's the expert," if it touched on something personal to us. I had other people, other interests in my life, where he had only me; of course he knew more about the way we worked, together or apart. Being bottled up must give you a great perspective. Ask a genie.

Perhaps I underestimate Small, how much he's learned by watching me at play with other people. Perhaps he would have known better how this game would go, if I had thought to ask him. I didn't do that, I was so determinedly living my own life now, even on our birthday; and so I was surprised by the silence, by the intensity in Quin as he moved those hands — hands like besoms, like bundles of loose-bound twigs — around the board. It was a good board, wooden and solid, but the pieces were cheap and hollow plastic, wholly incongruous in that setting or anywhere in that house. It took me a while, embarrassingly long to understand that they were wholly apt to his fingers, that they were light, easy to grip and easy to lift or slide. He could probably no longer handle the pieces proper to that board, with any comfort at all.

He could handle these pieces but not swiftly enough, or with sufficient purpose. I won in thirty-seven.

"Well," he said, fixing me with a gaze I couldn't read. "Kit, Michael might like another drink."

Anyone could have read that, it meant he wanted another game. Kit had been reading in a corner; the last ten moves, he'd come to stand behind me and watch. He said, "Surely. Anything you fancy, Michael. Champagne if you want it, for beating Quin."

"Actually," I said, starting to reset the pieces, white for my host, "I'd like another of those coffees, if I could."

"I knew you would. The mixture as before?"

"Please."

This time I did watch him make it. As he lifted one bottle into the light, I saw something bulbous stir in its depths, and had to bite back a cry; did it too slowly or not well enough, made noise enough to bring his head around.

"All right, Michael?"

"Yes, but — what is that?"

"Poire William. I said. Oh, you mean the pear? It's a pear."

It was. I could see it now that he'd named it: impossibly whole, bobbing in the liquor as Kit waggled the bottle from side to side. I wanted him to stop, and couldn't say so. Instead I asked the obvious, the moronic question, "How do they do that...?"

"They grow it there, of course. They have to. Can't cast a bottle around a pear, certainly can't squeeze it down the neck. Go out to the orchards in summer — if they have orchards, do they call them orchards if it's pears? — and you'd see all the pear-trees fruiting bottles. Feed the baby fruit into the neck while it's still tiny, tie the bottle to the branch and leave it there. I guess the bottle must have a greenhouse effect too, keep the insects off and help it ripen sweetly. When this bottle's empty, I'm going to break it open and have a taste, see what it's like inside. You want to share?"

I felt my whole face twitch and shook my head rapidly to hide it. "No, no thanks. Um, I'm not a fan of preserved fruit," which was a lie so direct, I thought so naked that I felt myself blushing as I said it, just to reinforce its flagrancy.

I turned back to the board in my confusion, to find that white's first move had been made already.

"I know you like to play the Ruy Lopez, which is unexpectedly old-fashioned of you. Let's see how you like to play against it."

Ordinarily not a problem, but my mind was full of

bottles, broken bottles, and my mouth tasted formaldehyde though I wasn't even drinking any more. I lost the game, and my lifelong undefeated status; and in twenty-nine moves, which was a capitulation.

"You'll stay for the decider," he said, not a question. "Play black again. We know you can beat me as white; I want you to do it the hard way. Concentrate, this time. No need to drink your coffee if you don't want to, but don't keep staring at it."

"Uh, sorry. Something on my mind."

"I know. One thing at a time. Bottle it up for now," which was maybe the worst way he could have found to say what he meant, but he wasn't to know that. Even chess isn't truly telepathic, which was how come I'd kept my crown so long, because Small couldn't really read my mind. Neither could Quin. Not yet, and not later. I was and am determined on that.

I took a sip from the disregarded mug and felt that same sweet, heavy, oily-bright bite, to work against what I wasn't really tasting, fear and formaldehyde; and I closed my mind down like shutters slamming, and I narrowed my gaze till it took in the chessboard and nothing more.

I can concentrate for England, if I have to. So could he. That game ran to fifty-three moves, and for the last twenty there was precious little left on the board to play with. Neither one of us suggested a draw; that would have been too easy, where there were still opportunities for both. In the end I was too savage or he was too subtle, or else his energy failed him, betrayed him, ran to me. He made a mistake, and I tore him apart.

And looked up then, finally, to find a stranger standing over us and oozing disapproval.

"Quin, you're doing too much and it exhausts you. Do I have to ration chess too?"

A big hand closed around a thin wrist, feeling for a pulse, but was shaken off abruptly.

"Don't make like a medic, leave that to Dr John. You wouldn't know what to do with a pulse if you could find it. And I have been rationed for months now, baby-chess, like a diet of Enid Blyton and tinned spaghetti. At last I find someone who understands, or at least plays better than I do. Him I can coach, and you're not taking him away from me. Michael, this is Gerard: never Mike, I gather, and never ever Gerry."

That same big hand reached for mine and folded itself around my fingers. I thought I could feel the effort he made, not to go for a bonecrusher grip.

"It's Michael's birthday," Kit said from the window, where he was apparently back on drinks duty, filling glasses. "Sixteen today. Yesterday," with a corrective glance at his watch.

"Is it indeed? Well, and how do you come to be here, Michael?" *Playing chess with my sick friend,* he meant, *exhausting him beyond the limits of his strength, when you should be off somewhere with your own friends and testing your own limits.*

"Uh, Kit found me out in the lane. I was going home but he brought me in, he knew I played chess and said Mr Quin would like a game," and never mind what else he'd said. If he could forget about that I was the last person to remind him.

Right at that moment it didn't matter what anyone else might have said. I'd clearly said something that was acting like acid on an ulcer, the room was so full of sudden twitches and sharp breathy sounds.

"If you're Michael," Kit said, "and Gerard is Gerard, then Quin is very definitely and always only Quin. If you mister him — well, actually, I don't know what would happen if you mistered him deliberately, I've never known anyone stupid enough to do it. One time brings the awful warning; after that, you're on your own. Cast into the outer darkness, probably, expunged from the family bible, I don't know. I just wouldn't go there, is all. See what I'm saying?"

I did see. I didn't understand, either Quin or Kit himself — why be a monosyllable where you can go the other way, why chop back when you can stretch out, accumulate, titles and honorifics and all the names in the book? — but adolescence is good cover sometimes for bewilderment. Unsure whether to apologise or to whom, whether to gloss over it or be casual, assume that same equality that Kit was proposing — "Quin, right you are, Quin it is," as easy as a grown-up — I came over all sixteen and said nothing at all.

And was rescued unexpectedly by Gerard's murmuring, "It's not that hard. Come on, practise; say 'Goodnight, Quin,' and get out of here. You too, Kit. Take your drinks with you. He's had enough for now."

Something in me expected Quin to protest like a child at bedtime, "one more game, I'm not tired yet," like that. In fact he only made a gesture, a little sweeping wave of his long hand that seemed to mean *he's right, take this board away and leave us be.* It was a beat later, still not too late that he smiled at me thinly and said, "Come back, Michael. Try me any time."

I nodded, and promised that I would. Kit said, "Later, Quin," moved the board off the bed and led me back to the kitchen.

"You get used to that," he told me, and it sounded like an invitation or a prophecy, *you will get used to that.* "He's sharp as a needle, and then suddenly he crashes. Gerard's the one who spots it, often as not, if he's around. You'd expect that, I suppose. I'm learning, but I still can't chase people out the way the big man does. He's the only one Quin listens to, anyway. You try saying 'Right, that's your lot,' when Quin's saying, 'Sit, stay, I'm not done with you yet.' It's not possible. I've all but given up trying."

I could imagine. I had been imagining, indeed, exactly that; it was only Gerard that I hadn't accounted for.

"You need more coffee?"

"No. Thanks, but I've not finished this," and thought I was not now expected to, thought I was on my way home.

"Not to worry, it's just as good cold on a warm night. Come through and sit for a while," out in the dog-room, the offshoot, where there were high wooden stools against a worktop. Kit perched; I subsided rather, down onto the floor next to the basket where Nigel's tail was thumping idly into his blankets. If I sat close enough I could put my arm round his neck and bury my fingers in the loose fur of his throat, while he could stretch over the basket's fraying rim to rest his chin on my thigh. We did that, then, and were both happy.

Kit gazed down on us with all the indulgent superiority he could contrive from his advantages of height and age, and said, "Smoke?"

"No. No, I don't, thanks." Well, I did, but not cigarettes, and not with almost-strangers.

"You should," he said, lighting up; and, "You will, if you spend much time round here. It's not strictly compulsory, but it's the mood of the moment, the spirit of the age. This has always been a smoker's house, and Quin's not allowed any longer, so it falls to the rest of us to keep up the average."

He seemed happy to carry his share of that burden. I watched the deep inhalation and the slow release, I watched his fingers roll the tip of the cigarette around an ashtray; eventually I said, "Kit?"

"Mmm?"

"How bad is Quin?"

"He's dying." And then, as though he was immediately conscious of the melodramatic weight of that, he tried to skip back from it: "I'm sorry, of course he's dying, you can see that. He's been dying for a long time, on and off. Only when he got sick this time, and it looks like being the last time, he just announces that he doesn't want to go into hospital again. Which leaves us, his loyal crew, to look after him. Somebody like Quin says something like that, you don't get a lot of choice. A few people slid off

into the undergrowth as soon as they saw we were serious,
but enough of us stayed around. It's not odorous. Actually
I take that back, sometimes it is odorous; I meant it's not
onerous, he doesn't own us," which was clearly a line he'd
used before, it came out way too slickly to be fresh.

"How do you know him, then?" Quin might have been
a full generation older than Kit before the sickness started
playing games with him, rubbing out his time-lines and
collapsing the softer structures of his face, making him
look older and younger both at once. Taking the same
game to extremes in his body, binding him to the bed like
a newborn, like an ancient, nothing like himself.

"All sorts of ways. Oh, me? I was his student. Under-
grad, postgrad, and he should have supervised my DPhil.
Well, he is, sort of, he gets to see it first. Just not officially.
But he was always my mentor, as much as my professor.
He said it just now, that he taught me everything I know.
That's not why I'm here, it's not a debt. A duty, maybe. I
do owe him, but this doesn't pay it off. I just come because
I have to, because I couldn't not. Most of us are like that,
I think: we loved him, and he needs us, so we're here. But
all the chess club backed away; and it's one of the things
he's got left that he can still do, one of the few, and none of
us can play to anything like his level. Which is why you're
so very welcome, Michael. It was such a lucky chance, us
finding you like that."

"Serendipity," I murmured, mostly because I still could.
"In the too, too solid flesh. But it was Nigel who found me."

"I suppose it was. Opening your presents. Do you want
to tell me about your brother, then?"

Did I want to? Probably not. But Small likes to be talked about, and my resistance was low. I nearly did take a cigarette when Kit offered for the second time, only my mug was empty by then and I didn't like smoking without a drink, that desert feeling as your mouth dries out; and I did absolutely tell the story, only I told it largely to Nigel. Maybe I overdid that. Or maybe it was the right thing to do, because when I was finished it gave Kit a way to go. Small can be such a dead end sometimes, a real conversation-killer.

"That's — unexpected," he said. "I thought — well, no, it doesn't matter what I thought. Accident, leukaemia, whatever. But when you said your twin was dead, I did think it might make this easier, introducing you to Quin. If you'd been there before, one way or another. Never mind. Big change of subject, or at least I think it's a change of subject. Michael, why don't you have a dog of your own?"

"I did," I said. "He died," and not such a change of subject after all, though no one had yet been crass enough to make the comparison. Except me, perhaps, and only in my head. Jack had been dependent on me too, and I was responsible for his death too, and he deserved to have his story told. Just not by me, not yet; I was still too guilty and too sore. Still hungry to suffer, my mother said, and she said I didn't deserve it. She tried to blame Small, and I wasn't having that. It was my fault, and I couldn't talk about it without accusing myself, and it was hard to do that without sounding disingenuous, as though I were fishing for an absolution that I really didn't deserve and didn't want. So I kept quiet or did the other thing instead, did this, dropped that single heavy word and let it lie, the whole melodrama shtick that Kit had ducked away from. If he thought I was doing it for its own sake, for the impact, let him think. His thinking couldn't hurt me, where I was hurt so much already.

"That's sad," he said; and there's no such thing as telepathy so I really have no idea what he was thinking, but *You see? You've been there before. One way and another*, all of that seemed to be implicit somehow, in his head or in mine. "Well, look, any time you want to borrow Nigel, just help yourself. Gerard won't mind."

"Gerard?"

"The big man, you just met him."

"Yes, but — um, his dog?"

"No, his house. Sorry, did you think he was just one of the team? He lives here."

"With Quin?"

"That's right. Absolutely with Quin. The rest of us come and go, but Gerard is constant. He's not big on dogwalking, though. Nigel is a sop to Quin and a burden to us all, so we'd be grateful. Brownie-points all round if you find time for Quin on top."

"Sure," I said. "I've always got time. And you don't need to be grateful." Nobody could lose here. They needed me, perhaps, a little; and what did I need more than time away from my mother, my brother, my self?

· · ·

Letting myself into a dark and unfamiliar house later than I'd reckoned and more drunk than I'd thought, being preternaturally cautious as I felt my way up the stairs, determinedly not talking to a dead brother nor to a dead dog when I might have done either of those things or I might have done both if I'd been sober and easy and at home, I found at the top that it had all been wasted effort, wasted silence, because my mother was awake and waiting for me, in bed but watching through her bedroom's open door.

"Michael. Come and talk to me. Did you boys have a good time?"

"Uh-huh." Perched on the edge of her bed and still wary, still feeling my way.

"Are you going to tell me about it?"

"Not much, probably."

"No, I thought — oh. Some things you can't hide. Let's see," and her bedside lamp snapped on and her hand touched my chin and turned my head to face her. "Hmm. Well, at least you didn't do it yourselves, with a needle and a candle and a cork. That was always our trick, and the holes always went septic. What does Small think about it?"

"I haven't asked."

"No. I think perhaps he'll let you know, regardless. Well, on your own head be it. Don't tell him I said so, but I think it looks fine. One stud, one ring — did Adam get the matching pair?"

"Of course."

"Good. I'm glad you have someone other than your brother, to share these things with. United by the smell of TCP, that's so sweet. How's your head going to feel in the morning?"

"I'll be fine."

"Fit for school?"

"Of course."

"Good boy. While we unpack, then. Go to bed now. Clean your teeth first, and drink a glass of water. And if you are suffering tomorrow, don't be too sixteen to say so. I've got plenty of nux vom."

VI

BEING SMALL

Small is not big into nux vom, or indeed anything else that I have to swallow. Nothing in, nothing out is his own chosen position, nil by mouth. He does understand how that wouldn't work for me, and he tolerates my eating — which is big of him, I think, I've always thought — but he still hates it when I medicate. I guess he's floating in the stuff himself, he reckons that's enough for both of us. Besides, I'm all the access he has to the world; he likes me clean and clear, a window, not a distorting lens disturbed by drugs or potions.

Self-medication, the same thing. He hates that too, when I'm drunk or doped up.

And I was right, he really really wasn't happy with the piercings. I lay sprawled on my bed while the room spun all around me and I felt adrift, afloat, a bubble of air in the swirl of the world, and his thin narky snarky voice went on and on in all the dizzy hollows of my skull.

He's short on resources, is Small, there's not much that

lies within his ambit; but what he lacks in reach he makes up for entirely in vitriol. Sometimes I think he's bathed in pure acid. Or else that he spits it, with a narrow focus and a lethal aim.

God knows, he's had the practice. One target, all my life. That thing that happens to you, where one line of a song gets stuck in your head and just repeats and repeats itself all day? Be glad of it, be grateful you're not me. I've read, I've been told how all kids thrill with horror at the legend of a worm that digs into your ear and chews its way right through to your living brain — but not me. I was born with him already in situ, and all my life he's been trying to chew his way out to open air.

No blame to him for that. Be fair; no one likes to be bottled up and kept in the dark. We'd all try to change that if we could. And I'm the lucky one, whichever way you want to count it. I owe him; I'm not denying that.

Just, I'm not sure that I owe him my life, the way he wants to claim it. My body's not his temple, any more than it is still his vehicle. I carried him around in my belly for long enough; I've carried him around in my head ever since; I think maybe that's enough. I don't have to be his mirror image, limited to what he makes of me, what he can match up to.

I wanted to put rings in my ears, and rings in Adam's too. I wanted THC in my system, TLC in my life. I wanted to come home drunk and topple into the room-spin and not have Small sit sour in my ear, all green and gooseberry.

I wanted time off for bad behaviour.

VII

CONSPICUOUS CONSUMPTION

School was for Mum, not for me. I was the instructor. It was how she tested what I'd learned, that I could teach her clearly and accurately, to have her understand. I didn't get to prepare the lessons; she said she knew all about my short-term memory already, there was little point in testing that. Spontaneity was the key, to find out how much I actually knew. She might ask for a lecture on particle physics, or else on metaphysics. Once she took me to the Ashmole and stood me in front of a Van Dyck deposition they have there, and had me talk to her about it. It was a Saturday morning; after twenty minutes I had a dozen random people listening in and the security people were getting restless, they thought it was some kind of student prank. I guess that was half the point of the lesson, to be sure that I was comfortable with an unexpected audience and the interventions of petty authority. These are the ways my mother thinks, inside and outside and all around the box.

Schooldays were necessarily weekends or bank holidays, to suit her working hours. Now she was on shifts, they were necessarily more various. Today was Friday; I was sixteen and one day old. We listened to Woman's Hour on Radio Four, that was sacred and inviolable, while I put together our infinitely adjustable shelving system, white-glossed bricks and scaffolding planks that we'd collected through the years. Then we both unpacked books, while I told her about glass: its chemical properties, its history and uses, the craft and the science and the art of it. That was an easy lesson. When I was eight, we'd lived next door to a man who worked with stained glass. I spent a lot of time hanging around his studio, learning from him, making little boxes with off-cuts of glass and lead and storing treasures in them. Sealing them up afterwards, folding over the seams of lead and storing them away. I had them still, as safe as the memories. I'd unpack them later, put them in a dark and private corner and never stop to wonder what was inside each, why I'd valued it then or why I kept it now. Treasures can be as secret as you like, and still have secrets of their own.

I ought perhaps to have tested my mother later, to see if the lesson stuck. She made such a point of keeping nothing, though, there'd be little point. Why should she hold on to this? Knowledge was my baby; I was hers. We both were, Small and I together, her specialist subject.

We lunched among the empty boxes, pasties and milk. Then she said, "I've got a shift at three. I just need to hunt out my work clothes, and that's me done for the day. Why don't you go for a run, get a feel for what's new around

here? Take your key, I'll be gone before you're back. Then
you can sort your own room out. You and Small will have
to look after each other tonight; it's my turn to be back
late, not till gone midnight. And Michael, I do mean
look after yourselves. Don't go bothering Adam tonight. I
know it's not a schoolday for him tomorrow, but neverthe-
less. He's got exams coming, he needs to buckle down.
No point winding his parents up, or rubbing his nose in
your freedom. Last night was a special occasion; don't try
to repeat it."

I only grunted at the lecture, but my heart leaped at
the idea of a run. It was what I was aching for, all thick
head and restless legs, the least worst residue of the night
before: less than I deserved, but I was dragging heavily
through the day. Just as well that she'd asked for a lesson
I could give without thinking. My temper was as brittle as
glass, and I guess my mood was as transparent. A morning
of my mother's close company was enough; I needed space
and time alone, fresh air and better exercise than shelves
and books and boxes.

I pulled clothes out of bags almost at random till I
found singlet and shorts and running shoes. Homer went
into a pocket and I was away, turning my face into the
wind, my feet up the hill. That was almost deliberately
perverse; downhill and downwind, there were parks from
here to the river. I could have done laps on grass, with
no traffic to watch out for. But I didn't want soft going,
underfoot or in my head. This was better, hard pave-
ments and hard work, legs and eyes and all my attention
given over to the thing itself, the running. Hot suburban

afternoon, there was none too much traffic, cars or people; I didn't always have to wait at street corners and I didn't always have to keep to the kerb, I could drop down and run on the road for stretches. Even so there were strollers and buggies and bikes on the pavement, there were parked cars and driven cars, occasionally a motorbike; there were traffic-lights and roundabouts where I had to keep aware.

And there was a map to make, to rediscover, to refresh: street names and grids and where the shops were, where the cops were, where the bus-stops and the cafes and the pubs. What had changed since last we lived this side of town, what was still the same and what eternal. I learned that little was eternal. Whole streets were gone. A church was now an architect's office, a '60s concrete council high-rise was fenced off and abandoned, barren, doomed. Some other landmarks seemed to have moved in my absence, shifting further north or east or simply crossing the road to face the other way. I took that as a salutary lesson, the best that I was fit for, that not even I was a reliable witness to my own life, and ran on.

Running and reading, refreshing, recording: they used me up, they left me nothing over. No space to store a hangover, no room for speculation. Perfect.

And when I'd run enough, when I'd had enough, I came back hot and drained and drifting, swimming in endorphins, happy as a lamb; and I stopped a few doors short of home, went with a whim, knocked on the back door of number thirty-nine and raised a volley of barking.

Raised footsteps too, a minute later. Raised a stranger,

a fat middle-aged man in a suit who gazed at me in all my sweat and exposure, cocked a quizzical eyebrow and said, "Can I help?"

"Uh, hi, my name's Michael, I was round last night..."

"Oh, yes. I read about you."

That made me blink, but I was still too short of breath for questions. Besides, Nigel had wormed his way through the man's blocking legs by then, all scrabble and lick and panting more than me. So I kept it short, just, "Can I borrow Nigel? Take him to the park for an hour?"

"With all my blessing."

"Brilliant. And, uh, if you could spare a drink of water, that'd be magic..."

He smiled, opened a fridge there in the offshoot and showed me how full it was of Volvic. "We use a lot of this," he said, passing me a chilly litre. "His lead's on the wall there. Don't let him loose on the road, he's got no sense of self-preservation. He doesn't run away from bad dogs, either, so you may have to save his life at great risk to your own; most of us have. Bring him back when you like, there's always somebody in and none of us will miss him while he's gone. My name's Brian, by the way. You'll see me again, I'm another regular on the rota here."

I wasn't sure how to take much of that, but it didn't matter. I had the dog, I had a drink, I needed nothing more. We went over to the park and I threw sticks and jogged and did a few stretches to show willing while Nigel chased sticks and butterflies and other dogs, made a hot and happy nuisance of himself but always came racing back to check on me, whether I whistled or not.

It's hard to whistle with a parched mouth. I swilled and spat, occasionally I tipped a chilly trickle over my head for the shiver of it as it dribbled down my back; mostly I sipped and swallowed, fighting the constant urge to gulp.

Thrifty as I could be, though, I still ran out too soon. Hot to the core, I was still sweating, and a litre of water couldn't touch the depth of my dryness. I stayed out as long as I could, for Nigel's sake and because I'd taken him and because there was so remarkably little to go back to.

Too soon for him, too late for me, I hauled him back to number thirty-nine. I rang the bell, and Gerard answered. I explained that I'd borrowed Nigel and was now bringing him back, and he said, "Thank you, we appreciate that. Are you coming in?"

"I'd better not. I'm all sticky, I've been for a run," and the sun must have baked me stupid if I could only say what was transparently obvious as I stood there in all my kit, with all my effort written on my body.

"Yes, I think I can see you steaming. I expect I could find a newspaper for you to sit on, if you're worried about our furniture. Alternatively, you're welcome to use our shower. Or the bath, perhaps? A cool bath on a hot afternoon?"

I felt my face change. Apparently I could hide nothing today. We didn't have a bath at Mrs Alleyn's, only a shower-room. A long slow soak, heat-sink and rehydration and the simplest of ancient pleasures all at once: I yearned for it and couldn't pretend otherwise, couldn't begin to stammer reasons why I shouldn't. Gerard laughed, took my elbow and steered me inside.

. . .

The bathroom was newly fitted out, almost industrial in scale. Much of that was for Quin's benefit, clearly: the door was wide enough for a wheelchair or for two men carrying a third, the bath had a lifting device built in, there were grab-handles everywhere. But the wall-to-wall tiling was as expensive as it was practical; the shower was a spectacular construct in stainless steel and too proud to contain itself in a cubicle or conceal itself behind a curtain, it just stood four-square in the room there above the green slate floor; the shelf above the bath had more ointments and unguents than I'd seen outside of Body Shop, and very few of them could even pretend to be medicinal.

Gerard slid a mirrored door aside, to show me towels behind. He said to take as long as I liked, Quin was asleep and there was another bathroom upstairs. Then he left me, and I went to lock that impressive door and found no way to do it.

Ah, well. He knew I was here, no doubt he'd tell anyone else who turned up. I stripped off while the bath filled, slid into the water, stretched out in purest contentment. It was almost deep enough to float me; I played with the taps until the temperature was exactly right, closed my eyes and drifted while the water soaked up heat and weariness

and what little temper I hadn't run off already. There must
be soap and shampoo among all those bottles above my
head, but no hurry for that, no hurry at all...

I was distantly aware of voices, footsteps going upstairs, coming down; then the door opened, and in walked
Kit.

I gaped at him; he smiled easily, and showed me what
he carried.

"Jeans and a T-shirt, when you're ready. We all keep a
change of clothes here, for when things get messy. These
are mine; it's lucky you're small."

"I am not...!"

The protest was instinctive, ritual, routine and too
swift to bite back, though I did try. He rolled his eyes
at his own clumsiness and said, "Damn. Sorry, that was
gauche. You're not big, though, and nor am I. These
should fit, and they're in much better taste than some of
the other choices you might have ended up with. Take
your time, though, I'm not trying to hurry you out. Fancy
a drink while you wallow?"

"What? Oh, no, no thanks. I'm fine..."

"No, you're not, you're just too shy to be waited on in
the bath. If you change your mind, shout. But — oh look,
this is ridiculous, you're not even trying. All this stuff is
here to use, you know."

And he came over and stood above me, picking
through the bottles on the shelf till he found something
green and glassy, uncorked it and tipped a stream of aro-
matic oil into the water.

"Don't panic, I won't swirl it around for you. Run a bit more hot in, though, to get the benefit. And relax."

"I was relaxed," I muttered, "till you came in."

That earned me a chuckle, and, "You can't be body-shy in this house, it doesn't work. The wet-room's communal, it has to be, sometimes we all need to clean up together. Or sometimes we just want to show off our tats. That's some scar you've got on your belly there, and you must be used to people looking. Don't tell me your school has shower-curtains in the changing rooms?"

"I don't go to school." I did go to public swimming-pools, but that was different. That was impersonal, and this was exactly not. And if I did get looked at, stared at there, it really was about the scar.

"Lucky boy. Well, you'll learn. We wander in and out, and don't think twice. These your sweats?"

Obviously they were, my singlet and shorts, nobody else had left their dirty running gear lying on the floor; and never mind that he'd brought me other clothes to wear, I still yelped as he scooped them up, and he still laughed at me as he felt through the pockets of the shorts, found Homer and fished him out.

"I'm just putting a load through the machine now, they may as well go in with the rest. If they're not dry before you go home — well, who cares? You weren't going to put them on again tonight."

Which meant I could borrow his gear till the morning. I was grateful, and embarrassed; and out of my depth and all at sea and all sorts of watery metaphors, and suddenly there seemed to be nothing I could do but close my eyes and gulp a breath and let my body slide down that deep, deep bath until the clear waters closed above my head.

. . .

I lay there as long as I could, trying not to think of parallels, of bodies naked and preserved, observed in liquids. *I am not small, I am not Small* — but the words were slithery and hard to keep a grip on, and eventually I had to give up, to let go, to surge up out of the water gasping and blinking and shaking my head against the ringing in my ears.

Kit wasn't there, of course. Nobody was, just this great puddle that I'd spilled out of the bath. I groaned, and wondered who would realise if I mopped it up with a towel — and then watched the water slip with a sense of purpose across the slates, till it found a drain I hadn't noticed in the corner. Stupid of me. There was a shower, right out in the open there; there had to be a drain. A wet-room, Kit had called it, and now I understood why. I could splash as much as I liked, spray water all around the walls, it'd all just run off and drain away.

Another day, in other company, that might have been fun. Right now, I was nervous just standing up to find soap and shampoo on the shelf, with my back to that unlockable door. *Relax*, he'd said, but even in the saying he'd stolen any chance of it.

Maybe he was right, maybe I would learn. I did hope so. In the soft lights of a luxury bathroom, the grudging little cubicle in Mrs Alleyn's eaves was losing any brief attraction it ever might have held. In the meantime I washed quickly, hopped out and scuttled for the safety of a towel.

Hasty drying, with both eyes on the door and willing it not to move, not to open even a fingernail's width till I was decent, and I wriggled damply into Kit's jeans. No underwear: that was novel, interesting, not uncomfortable. The jeans were maroon with fraying sea-green seams, rotted to rags at the cuffs, a snugly comfortable fit. The T-shirt was a faded coral, still holding its shape but way too wide across the shoulders, so that the sleeves hung down past my elbows. Kit had one of those bantam-cock bodies, neat and strutty, broad above and narrow below. I guessed that the jeans must have been his party trousers before they were retired: exhibition-tight, denim doing lycra's job.

I used a corner of the towel to scrub condensation off the mirror, just to see. My own clothes were all cheap and baggy, street fashion because that was easiest, and mostly black. Black gone to grey, mostly. Unless my mother chose them: she'd dress me in colours when she could, but not like this.

And that's how Kit found me, of course, when he quietly slid the door aside and came back in. In front of the mirror, not preening but looking, yes, and liking.

"Oh, you're out already. I was just bringing you that drink you didn't think you wanted," and he waved a glass gently, tall and shimmering with bubbles, ice, a wedge of lemon. Thoroughly moistened outside, I was startlingly dry again within, and suddenly craving. Which he saw and laughed at even as he set the glass down in a soap-dish, by the shower and out of my reach.

"One more minute, let me look at you first. Stand still."

He twitched the towel from my nerveless fingers and rubbed briskly at my hair, two-handed; then he went to the shelf, twisted the top off a flat grey pot and took out a fingertip's-worth of something that he slapped between his palms as he walked back to me.

"What's that?"

"Clay," he said, all matter-of-fact as he worked it lightly into my hair.

"Really clay?"

"Really. Dug by virgins with silver spoons by moonlight, I expect, the price we pay."

"From the banks of the sacred river Alph?"

"That's the one," and now his smile was less teasing and more fraternal. Only his fingers teased lightly, twisting and lifting; and then it was all satisfaction, that smile, and he wiped his hands on the towel where he'd left it hanging over my shoulder, and he turned me round to face the mirror again and said, "Better?"

It wasn't a question. He knew already. My hair looked wild, slept-on, in a good way. Freshly-towelled might be a better way to say it, but ready to stay so for the rest of the night. And the earrings glittered gold against that dark unkemptness and I liked that too, it was new too but a different newness, a different voice against this rush of strange; and I wanted to keep the clothes, worn as they were, and of course I couldn't say so because of course Kit would just say *do it*. I daren't even be too effusive in my thanks. I'd only known these people twenty-four hours; there was a generosity in them that I distrusted deeply. Unless it was myself that I distrusted, or my brother. Our ability to reciprocate. We were neither of us any good at giving things away.

But if I couldn't be open-handed for fear of his filling them with gifts, I could at least not be mean-spirited. I smiled at him through the mirror, or rather I shrugged off all my caution and let him see what lay beneath, how simple my pleasure was.

"Good." His hands were still on my shoulders; he turned me again, towards the door this time. And whisked the towel away, and said, "Pick up your drink, and go see Quin. He's expecting you."

"Gerard said he was asleep ... "

"That was then, this is now. He sleeps; he wakes. It's a pattern. Get used to it. Go."

. . .

There was gin in the glass, but not too much. It was mostly tonic, ice-cold fizz with a bite to it, perfect. I sipped as I went, down the passage and not hurrying, taking the chance to linger, to browse the titles in the bookshelves; and so slowly to Quin's door, which stood open.

Music was leaking out, distantly familiar, eerie voices riding a woodwind thread over percussion. I was snared by that, drawn on almost without thinking, inside almost before I understood that I was moving.

Quin was in the bed, of course, and propped up as I'd

seen him yesterday. Gerard was in a chair at the foot of the bed, not close. For a moment that looked odd, but then I thought not. Easier for Quin to see him, he didn't have to turn his head. They were too comfortable with each other, these two, they didn't need to be touching-handy.

Nor did they need to be talking, apparently, even with their eyes. Gerard had his closed, Quin's were turned upward to the ceiling; they sat in each other's eyeline, but not under each other's eye. They were both listening to the music, but independently so.

That seemed to be how they lived their lives, too. Or at least how Gerard lived his life and Quin his half-life, his encroaching death. Sometimes I wondered what that must be like, to face the world solo. Solo but supported, which was different again, perhaps better again. In this house everyone was individual, undivided; and no one carried anything alone.

Do I sound jealous?

Perhaps I felt jealous. Even of Quin, perhaps, on his big bought-in deathbed there, with all his guardians about him. Especially of Quin, perhaps. I knew too much about survival to envy Gerard what he had to come. That was the label I'd worn all my life, what the scar said, some part of what I had to carry: that I was the living twin, the only twin, the strong one. Secretly, some part of me had always fancied being Small instead.

I stood just inside the doorway, gripped by that music and that moment. After a minute Quin saw me, attracted I think by my stillness, by my utter determination not to move.

"Michael," he said. "Come and sit."

"I don't want to disturb you."

Gerard opened his eyes. "We may be quiet, but we're not in church. Come in, sit down, talk to us. It's all right, we've heard this piece before."

So had I, but I had to come at it backwards. Something about war and a poet, but not war-poetry, and not English ... Drama and death, plenty of death ... Ah. Federico Garcia Lorca, I'd spent a week on him once: reading his work and his biographers', following some links and finding others. There'd been movies made and ballets, music written. Song cycles, from his poetry ...

"George Crumb," I said. "*Ancient Voices of Children.*"

Gerard's eyebrow twitched. "I'm impressed. This was big for us in the seventies, but I didn't think it was still in the repertoire. Or did you peek?" with a nod towards the CD case where it lay by the stereo.

"No. I heard it once, a while back."

"Just the once?" That came from Quin.

"Uh, yes. I was into Lorca for a bit," *for a week* but I didn't want to say that, "so I chased up everything I could. And, well, I've got this freak memory. I don't forget much."

Actually it was Small who had the memory, my pocket elephant, my spare hard-drive. I could outsource my experience, safe in the knowledge that he hoarded everything. No use saying "Forget it," not to Small; he never would, and he never would let me.

"That must be convenient," Gerard suggested.

"I suppose. It's just normal, I live with it."

"Sounds like hell to me," Kit said cheerfully,

unexpectedly at my back. Focused on the music and its sources, I hadn't heard him coming.

"That's because you do nothing worth remembering, and plenty that you crave to forget," Gerard said dryly.

"Plenty that I drink to forget. Michael, never stand between a man and the drinks tray," as he pushed me further into the room, and down into a chair. "Do you need a top-up? No, you don't. Help yourself when you do, I'll be in the kitchen. Tea's in an hour. Just the four of us, yes?"

"Oh — no, not me, you don't have to ..."

"Of course I don't have to, but I will. If you'd like to stay. Yes?"

"Well — yes, then. Please. Thank you."

"You're welcome."

I hoped that was true. I hadn't been angling for an invitation, any more than I'd angled for a bath, and I didn't want them thinking so. On the other hand, images of last night had been brightly in my mind, set against the likely reality this evening, sorting bags and boxes while I chewed on whatever food I could find, what Mum had thought to bring with us or buy in. Determined not to gatecrash, I had none the less deliberately put myself in their path here, done them the favour with Nigel, given them the opportunity to be grateful if they chose.

I thought there'd be another price to pay. I thought Quin at least would be safe to extract one. I didn't trust his smile; I thought he was reading me like a book. But then, I thought that all human relationships were like this, a series of mismatched trade-offs, favours and IOUs,

shifting debits and credits with each side keeping their
own tally and none of the figures audited. I didn't see how
the world could work otherwise, what would ever keep
it turning. You always had to be leaning forward, a little
off-balance, trying to get ahead.

Only Quin didn't need to do that anymore. He lay
queen-like at the centre of his particular court and everyone danced attendance on him, and he could never, never
think to pay them back.

Reminded me of someone, couldn't think who.

I sipped gin with no thought of a refill, content to
make this last; I listened to the music, and watched the
two men do the same. Or do it differently, rather: they
knew what I only remembered, and there's an order of
magnitude between.

The chessboard lay at my elbow. I could offer Quin a
game when the music finished, show willing. I thought
he'd say, though, if that was what he wanted. I thought
that was how this household worked, that they all de-
ferred to Quin in his decay, because that was what he
would expect.

Let him say, then. One way or another, I expected to
sing for my supper. I'd be disappointed not to. A bath
and a supper left me lagging, in their debt despite the
dogwalk; I wanted to go home ahead, netting brownie-
points against tomorrow. At the very least, I wanted to
feel that I was in the game.

I thought Quin knew that; I thought I'd get the
opportunity.

. . .

No chess that day. I wanted not to suggest it, not to seem to push my only claim on his company. He might have offered, only that someone else came while the Crumb was still echoing in our heads, in the silence of the room.

This guy was in his thirties, and he greeted the two men with a kiss each, me with a friendly nod. His name was Tony; he settled into a chair, saying, "I know I'm early, but I cleared it with Kitty in the kitchen, she's putting another pint of water in the soup. I've had such a day, I couldn't tell you ..."

"Do try," Gerard said. Dryly, I thought. Quin gave him a look.

"Well, I will, but bear with me. I'm good for nothing. It started at eight, can you believe it? Eight o'clock in the morning, and this client calls up in a tizz. On the mobile, if you please, I could have been anywhere with anyone and doing anything; and she knows I'm never myself before midday. Oh, you bitch, I thought, take your mind off your dick for one minute and think about someone else's, can't you? But no, she has to be serviced, then and there. So I'm down to the office with nothing inside me but a cold swill of last night's coffee, and we have a crisis meeting over what's really not a crisis at all, she's just getting antsy about the numbers. Well, some people do get scared when you get into seven figures. So I crunch them up for her, and she goes home happy, and I really wish I could have done the same; only by then there were three appointments waiting, and ..."

And cutting through all the words and all the posturing, he was a high-powered accountant whose day had been much like most of his days, I thought, except that he was making an exhibition of it to amuse Quin, or possibly himself. I felt excluded, redundant, resentful; and was already on my feet and making an awkward exit, trying to pretend I was browsing the bookshelves for simple interest's sake and hey look, the books were leading me out into the passage when he produced a paper from his shoulder-bag and said, "And I didn't even get to finish the crossword, for God's sake! You'll help, won't you? Listen, R blank E blank S and three blanks —"

"Rheostat," I said, before he could read out the clue. And made my exit on the word, far more dynamically, and closed the door behind me without looking back and only hoping that I was right, so that he could mutter, "Rheostat, rheostat ... God, he's right, you know, he is right. Has he done the *Guardian* already? He must have, mustn't he? Did you do it here? And who is that boy, anyway ...?"

And then let them say what they liked, I couldn't hear it. I was in the kitchen, helping Kit.

· · ·

Helping is a flexible concept. I asked if there was anything I could do; he threw the question straight back at me. "I don't know. *Is* there anything you can do?"

"Not much," despite my sterling efforts to teach my mother how to cook for me. You can't teach what you don't know.

"Fair enough. There's no room for two anyway, unless they're lovers. Even then, this kitchen can lead to divorce. I've seen it happen. You feed the hound, then sit in the offshoot with the door open and we'll talk like Pyramus and Thisbe. Get yourself a refill before you go. In the corner there, chef's perks. Easy on the gin, mind, there's wine later. Did Tony scare you out?"

"Not scare, but..."

"... But he came on too strong for your tender blood. *I* know. I couldn't abide him, first off. You do get used, though. You just have to hear the irony, cutting through the camp. Or hear him talk to a client. I've seen him on the phone; he turns it down to an ice-edge, but all the time he's mugging furiously to us, queening it up like a panto dame. That's it, it's all performance. He only does it to annoy. Just don't get annoyed, and you'll be fine."

"I think I might have annoyed him."

"That works too. The boy has resources. Nigel, out of the kitchen, thank you very much. You too, Michael. This is a demonstration, not a masterclass — we'll do hands-on, but later."

· · ·

So I perched on a stool in the doorway and watched him cook. Cubes of pork with green beans and spring onions, in a cream and mustard sauce; if not a masterclass it was absolutely a lesson for me, and I did learn. In my life, garlic came dry in granules, and you shook them from a jar. Of course I knew about cloves and bulbs and garlic-presses, which was why we would never have fresh garlic, because my mother didn't run to gadgets. More trouble than they were worth, she said, just think of the washing-up. Perhaps it was a consequence of the migratory life we led, from kitchenette to primus stove to someone else's kitchen, but my mother's definition of a gadget seemed to run far and wide. She allowed a couple of battered saucepans, good for heating what came from tins; she did have a huge old frying-pan, for the all-day breakfasts that were her fallback position. Not much else.

Not like here. Here the kitchen was full of devices. Many of them looked new, but not unused. Kit did his cooking with a chopping-board, though, and a knife: which was how I learned that a garlic-press isn't crucial after all, that the edge and the flat of a knife are all you need to address a clove of garlic.

"Pretty much all you need, full stop," Kit averred, when I said that aloud, or something like it. "Give me a knife, a spoon and a pair of chopsticks, and I will travel the world. Don't look so worried, I won't make you eat with chopsticks tonight. I think I will cut everything up good and small, though. Fork-food, easy to manage. Whoever cooks gets to clean up after, that's a house rule. And we all eat with Quin, that's another; and it's been a while since he made it to the dining-room. Gerard uses that as a study these days, the table's all buried under papers. So we eat off our laps, and I can live without spillage."

He fried cubes of cold cooked potato in butter, scattered them with parsley, divided everything up into huge white bowls. He told me to start carrying through to the front room, while he took a dish of dark brown jelly out of the fridge, scooped a ladleful into another bowl and began to chop it into neat little dice.

"What's that?"

"Consommé, for Quin. It's about all he can stomach at the moment. Luckily, he likes it. But then, who wouldn't? Concentrated gravy, essence of beef with red wine and brandy for added bite: it's like a whole Sunday dinner in a spoon, without all the bother of chewing. Want to try?"

He ran his finger round inside the ladle, and it came up with jelly clinging. I thought he was going to hold the finger out, for me to lick; but he slid it into his own mouth instead, and offered me the ladle. *Monkey see, monkey do.* So I did, and then I trotted back and forth with bowls and napkins, glasses and forks and wine while this dark, intense sliver of pure savour melted slowly and secretly on my tongue.

· · ·

"Royal jelly," Tony said, when he saw Quin's supper. "Serve up enough of it, it turns a grub into a queen-bee."

"Am I that grubby?" Quin sucked consommé off a teaspoon, slowly. "And do you mean fat and pale, or just unsanitary?"

"Neither of those, any more. You're in transition. Which is why you have your drones," and a sweep of his glass included all of us, "buzzing about you."

"Tony," Gerard said, "be quiet, and fetch another bottle."

"I'll go," I said quickly, getting to my feet and halfway out of the door already, half my mind on second helpings, the scrapings in the pan.

Behind me, I heard, "I like that boy," and "Mmm, so do we, we thought we might adopt him," and "For the duration."

They spoke softly, but I could still put a name to each of the three voices. The first was Tony's, and the second Kit's. The third — well, I'd heard that exchange before. Last time had been in the woods, and Peter had said it, but he wasn't here. This time it had come out acid, and was Quin's.

. . .

Whoever cooks gets to clean up after. I insisted on helping with the washing-up, just to cement my claim. But then I went home, virtuously early. Tony had disturbed the evening's flow, and there'd be no chance of extra brownie-points tonight. It was hard to leave, but I'd had as much as I'd hoped for, more; and not to overstay my welcome in the one house, not to let that welcome cause me trouble in the other, both of these were important. By the time my mother came in most of my things were in my room and I was in my bathrobe, and my breath smelled of nothing but spearmint and scrubbing.

. . .

Saturday morning I put on my own clothes, old clothes, and remembered that I'd forgotten to reclaim my running gear, damp or dry; and looked at Kit's clothes and wondered if I should wash them. By hand, that would have to be, and laboriously in the basin, and drying them above the bath and fielding questions from my mother, whose were they and why had I been wearing them? It wouldn't last, but just for now I found that I quite liked it, to have a part of my life that she couldn't interrogate.

So I folded Kit's things as neatly as I could manage and put them in a bag as they were. One evening's wear on a fresh-bathed body, I hadn't spilled anything and I hadn't been close while he was cooking; I didn't think they smelled, of garlic or of me.

My mother took me on an expedition to the local shops, before she went back to work. I kept my eye on number thirty-nine as we passed, but there was no sign of life. Quin's curtains were closed, and Kit's car wasn't in the driveway. We found the library, with its free broadband access for registered ticket-holders; that was my school, one of my schools, and she gave me a task and left me there to pursue it.

Blood, she said, *learn about blood.* She didn't need to say more. From the discovery of pulmonary circulation to the latest advances in haematology, all the knowledge in the world was out there, and the hunt was up.

I wondered sometimes whether she had any plan for

my education. If there were a logical progression from subject to subject, I could never see it; she seemed to pluck these projects at random from what she knew or what she thought I ought to know, wherever she thought some new branch of learning might lie. Sometimes they seemed strangely appropriate, as now, significant almost — but the world is a web of links, and all things interconnect. The true surprise would be if she managed to produce a series that was truly random, unaffected by her life or by mine. And with subjects so broad, so fundamental, how could they not apply?

If there were a goal to all this study beyond the thing itself, I couldn't see that either. If there were an end-point, she had never said. College seemed unlikely, unless I proposed it myself. I supposed I should make that decision soon, one way or the other. There would be public exams, no doubt, that I would need to sit and pass. Or if I decided against, again no doubt she was waiting for me to say so, to say *no more learning now, it's time I got a job* or *time I travelled, time I left home* or *my turn to look after you.*

This much at least I knew about myself, that I didn't make decisions easily or well. I could leave it to Small to choose for both of us; that might be best. Otherwise, I'd have to choose for him. That might not work out too well, for either one of us.

I had my hour on the net, then spent a while longer with the online catalogue, planning a strategy, a route into understanding, and tagging books I'd need to borrow. In a week, I should be able to answer any questions she might have for me; but a week's study would only throw up questions of its own, mapping the depths of what we didn't know. I could be a month on this road, easy, if she left me to follow it so long. She rarely did. I think she was frightened of speciality, of obsession. She knew how tight my focus could go, and how long I could walk a line.

How long's a piece of string, Michael?
As long as you let it be. How long can I have?
As long as Small allows it.

That really was the way it worked, the way we worked it out between the three of us. If I'd been a thief, she'd have given us just enough rope for Small to hang me. She felt safe to let me run, because she knew she could rely on Small to rein me in again, because he always did. *Twins watch out for each other*, she used to say that often, until neither one of us needed to hear it anymore.

Which was maybe why I didn't want to tell her about my ongoing adventures at number thirty-nine. Her interest would pique Small's jealousy, which would bring not an end but an immediate limit to those adventures, *thus far and no further: she lets you out and I pull you back, you know you can't be trusted by yourself.*

I knew he didn't trust me out alone, which might or might not be the same thing. But as long as our mother didn't know, then we were in collusion, Small and I, and that was a different thing entirely. Twins need to share their secrets, or what was ever the point of being twinned?

I found a bakery and bought a couple of cheese pasties, munching as I walked back to the house. It was another sunny day, we were having a run of them, it almost amounted to a summer; maybe I'd take a book to the park. Maybe I'd take a book and a dog.

Kit's silver Mini was parked in the lane, because their drive was full of cars. I went home, washed crumbs and grease off my face and fingers, did the best I could with my hair, collected my book and the bag of Kit's clothes and headed straight out again.

Confidently up the drive and round to the back of the house, squeezing by all the cars; a confident ring on the offshoot doorbell, the usual blizzard of barking and Nigel's happy feet against the woodwork; a long wait, longer than usual, longer far than you'd expect. Long enough, eventually, to have me ringing again. And then cautiously opening the door, knowing that it was never locked; sticking my head inside the offshoot and calling out, "Hullo?"

No answer, but I could hear voices dimly, thickly, faded by distance and roughened by the walls and doors between us, all but drowned altogether by Nigel's noise. I quieted him as best I could and went up to the door into the house proper. And knocked there, much less confident now; and was just on the turn, just wanting not to be heard after all so that I could slip away and be gone and pretend I never came, when I saw a figure through the dimpled glass.

The door opened, and it was Gerard. The big man, all in his shirtsleeves, no tie but his good suit trousers that he hadn't had time to change; and there was blood on his white shirt and blood on his hands, a spray of blood across his face and glasses and he snapped, "Oh, for the love of God, boy, not now!"

"No, right, sorry, only I brought Kit's clothes back ..."

"What? Did you? Oh, I see," as I waved the bag at him vaguely. "Don't give it to me," showing me his hands, "leave it on the counter there and go away."

And then he was gone and the door had slammed behind him.

• • •

I stood still for a minute, just thinking; and the easy thought, the obvious thought was that nobody in that house would have time for Nigel now. Hadn't had for a while by the look of him, not fussing at me but just whining at the back door now, scratching at it where the scars showed he had scratched a lot before.

So I put the bag of clothes on the counter there, just where I'd been told to, and I took Nigel's lead down off the wall where it was hanging, and I took him out for a walk.

For a good long walk, we went all the way down to the river and a fair distance along, he was tired and lagging before I let him lead me back; and when we reached the house again I let him in quietly, checked that he had water, hung up the lead and went away. The clothes had gone; I hoped that they'd proved useful.

• • •

Adam phoned, to talk about his yesterday's hangover and hold out an unspoken willingness to face the same tomorrow. I deliberately didn't hear the implicit invitation, knowing that he couldn't spell it out. As the free one and the wicked one, it was my task to lay temptation in his path, his to succumb. He needed someone to blame, and not himself. Between us, Small and I could ordinarily soak up all the guilt that was going, but not tonight. Tonight I was all full and we wanted time alone, Small and I.

When my mother came home, brightly questioning, I told her about my quiet day: work in the library, a long walk in the afternoon and home all evening. Perhaps an early night, I said, take my book to bed. She smiled over teenage constitutions and how there might be a timelag but a night's indulgence would always catch up in the end; she asked if I wanted a milky drink, and waved me goodnight when I said no, and told us not to lie awake half the night with the radio on.

· · ·

We lay awake half the night with the radio on, too quiet for her to hear. Sometime around midnight I heard a dog being walked in the lane outside. For a little while the footsteps were silent and the dog was not, barking inquiringly, impatiently. I lay still, didn't turn a light on, didn't look out of the window. Soon enough the footsteps moved on, and the dog went with.

· · ·

Next day I kept close to my comforts: staying indoors and setting my room up the way I liked it, everything placed where it always was, where I knew it ought to be. Books went into alphabetical order by subject, starting in my own room and winding through to the living-room, on their brick-and-scaff-plank shelving. CDs did the same, and then my mother's old LPs that she couldn't or wouldn't replace. Lunchtime came and went but I was busy, too busy to go out or to scavenge for whatever food there was in the flat. Not hungry, anyway. All day I'd been drinking too much coffee; I was jittering, restless, flitting from one project to another, reading a page here and writing a paragraph there and then finding something else to do.

I was hoovering the stairs when the doorbell rang. Nice and handy to answer, it might almost have been deliberate, I might almost have been hanging around waiting, anticipating, filling time.

Who knew where we were, who'd got caught up with our new address? Adam, of course, but it was a school day and he wasn't a skiver in the easiest of times. With exams upcoming, he'd be diligent even without his parents' pressure. My mother's work, but she was there right now and they didn't make housecalls anyway. My mother's friends? Perhaps, but they were trained to telephone before they came; her shifts were too erratic to predict and I'd had enough of stilted conversations with the middle-aged.

It could have been Mrs Alleyn, of course, with a cake or a complaint for her new tenants. It could have been a postman with a parcel. It could have been —

— but it was not. This door too had panes of dimpled glass in its upper quadrants to give a darkling view of who stood on the step, that odd compromise gesture between privacy and security. I could see, not clearly but all too well.

Which if it was true for me, it was true or true enough for him also. He didn't have the advantage of seeing me in a fall of sunlight, as I did him; but who else could I be, my size and shape in the shadows of the hall here, and demonstrably not my mother? He'd know. If my fingers hesitated at all on the latch of the door, it was barely measurable, I barely knew it myself and he couldn't possibly.

"Hullo, Kit."

He hadn't brought Nigel. If I had thought he'd come at all, I'd have thought he might come with Nigel. "Michael. Don't ask me in, hon, I can't stop; it's my shift, and Peter wants to get away. I'm just here on an errand. Two errands, actually. The first is to bring you these back," and he swung a carrier bag into my arms, heavy with fabric and oddly warm, "and the second is to act as spokesperson for an older generation. Gerard asked me to apologise to you — well, no, not that, Gerard never apologises and he wouldn't get me to do it for him, but he did say that he feels badly. He was short with you yesterday and you took the dog out anyway, and we are grateful."

"He doesn't have to apologise."

"Just as well," with a bright blond smile, "because he isn't going to, and he'd kick me halfway to kingdom come if I tried to pretend that he was."

"No, really. What's to apologise for? Something bad

was happening, and I turned up out of the blue, and he just —"

"— couldn't be bothered with you? That's the point. He has a grand grasp on the essentials, and a fine talent for discourtesy on the side. You did pick a bad time; when Quin starts leaking like that it's all hands to the pump and damn the torpedoes. We wouldn't have answered the door at all if he hadn't been in the kitchen anyway for a bowl of water and some J-cloths. And you couldn't have come in even if you'd wanted to, you've got to know what you're doing and you don't; but he says he was abrupt and he regrets that, and he doesn't want you to misunderstand. So he says, will you come out to dinner with us tonight? Just the three of us, I think, unless someone else turns up in the meantime."

"He doesn't have to ..."

"No, of course not. Which is why you should say yes, because the offer's genuine. And if you don't, he'll either think you're sulking or else that he's scared you off altogether, and either one of those would be a pity, and really hard to work your way back from."

He was right, of course. I could find any number of easy excuses — *I need to stay in and work* or *stay in and unpack, I really ought to eat with my mother tonight* or else *go out with my friend* — and they all had the advantage of being true; but what he said was equally true, and number thirty-nine was still too new and too interesting, I wasn't ready to lose it yet.

I needed a gracious way to say that, and looked in the bag to find it, the way you do, occupying hands and eyes with mundane things while your brain is scrabbling; and was suddenly arrested by a glimpse of unexpected colour, red and green, his old faded jeans nestling in among my running clothes.

I put my hand in and pulled them out, soft and warm, washed and freshly ironed. "These are yours."

"Not any more, sunshine. Not if you want them. I was glad to have them last night, something to change into; but they deserve better and they're too tight on me now, I can't wear them out in public any more. And you looked so cool the other night, pattering in and out with drinks and dishes like some cute little houseboy all dressed up to party ... You don't need the T-shirt, but I do think you need to have these. Wear them to dinner tonight. Seven o'clock: just come to the door and we'll drive, I guess. I don't know where we're going, he hasn't said, but it won't be jacket-and-tie for us. If we dress down, he can feel dressed up, and that's more comfortable for everyone."

. . .

At seven o'clock, anxiously punctual, I was walking up their drive in my best new birthday shirt and Kit's trousers that were my own trousers now, that I'd sidled out to stop my mother seeing. I was fresh from the shower, and my hair was still damp; I'd tried for that rough-towelled look again, only it wasn't going to last however hard I tweaked and tousled at it now.

The offshoot door was open. I rang the bell anyway

and stepped inside. No volley of barking, no dog dancing on my newly-scrubbed trainers; I was worried instantly. An open door and no Nigel might spell trouble. A whistle in the street, any casual whistle and he'd be off, and did he have the sense to find his own way home?

Kit, at the inner door: he gave me a smile for the trousers, a nod for the shirt, a frown for the hair and a quick gesture, *come in, be quiet...*

I swallowed my questions and was quiet, went in. And followed him through the house to Quin's room, and had my questions answered with a glance. Quin was in the bed as ever, but Nigel was on it, stretched out in luxurious contentment with his head on Quin's thigh. Both of them were asleep; one was snoring gently, only that I wasn't quite sure which.

Brian was sitting in a chair by the window. He had a book face-down in his lap, a glass in his hand. He gave me a nod, and touched his finger to his lips.

A tug on my sleeve; I was led away, down the passage to the bathroom. Once the door was closed:

"That's a special treat," Kit said softly. "As we're going out."

"Treat for which one?" They both looked fairly happy about it.

"For us, obviously. We don't often see him sleeping like that. It sends us on our way happy, and with luck we get to keep Gerard amused for a couple of hours without him even thinking about ringing home. You have to eat slowly, all the way through the menu, as many courses as you can and coffee after."

Fine, I could always eat. My mother starved me. And I was eating for two, I kept telling her that, and all she did was clout me.

"Oh, and talk too, you have to talk. He's heard too much of me, I'm only there as a makeweight, not to leave you feeling spooked. You can talk about Quin if you want to, he doesn't mind that. Just don't let him brood. He's too broody, and that's not good for anyone, him or Quin or anyone. Good, your hair's still wet ..."

He'd learned that by playing with it, all without my consent. Now he fetched his pot of sacred clay and fixed it for me, again without any suggestion that I might have a voice in this.

Like the last time, I thought it looked grand when he'd finished. So I thanked him, while he washed his hands; he said, "You need something to feel good about. And you're sixteen, so we may as well keep it simple. If you look good, you can feel good."

As I went into the lion's den, he clearly meant. Sixteen, and a job of work to do. "I thought this was about him making it up to me?"

"From his point of view, it is. I'm just co-opting you into a conspiracy. It shouldn't be that awful, anyway; Gerard can be intimidating, but he's fun once you break him down. He disapproves of me, which is terrific. Only I've played that about as far as it'll comfortably stretch, and someone else has to make the running now. Tonight, my sweet Michael, that someone is you. Not a sacrificial victim, just a resource. Not even a fresh titbit for a jaded palate; the looking pretty is for your pleasure, not for his."

Maybe, but I felt like a titbit all the same. He'd fed me to Quin because I played chess, and now he was feeding me to Gerard because — well, because he could, because I was there, because the need was there and the opportunity arose.

"Okay," I said, "but I'm keeping the clay." He'd said it himself, those little pots came expensive.

"Sure," he said, "it's yours, only it stays here. Drop in and use it, any time. Door's always open," and he opened the bathroom door as he said it and said, "Here's Gerard," in exactly the same easy voice.

And here was Gerard coming down the hallway: big man, dressed to impress but not, I thought, to impress me. You don't put on a suit and tie to build fences with a teenage boy. He gave me a nod and half a smile, "Glad you could come, Michael," and then turned to Kit. "Are we ready? I thought the Mokhtar."

"I thought you might. Is that the closest you can come to informal? It's fine with me, but I'm not the guest of honour. Michael? You like Indian?"

"Yeah, sure."

"Good. We all like the Mokhtar. Most of us go there for the food, which is fabulous. Gerard goes for the starched linen and the stiff service, a punkah-wallah in every booth and all the fans wafting the odour of the Raj, which they've preserved in bottles since 1923."

"Kit, if you can't behave I'll leave you behind." His voice was mild enough, but his glasses flashed blankly dangerous. Kit didn't even blink.

"Oh, I'll behave. The question is, how will I behave?

Behaviour's like weather, it's like the poor, it's always with us."

"And so are you." Longsuffering was scored into every short snapped word, but I thought that was deliberately done. Just as I thought that Kit was needling him deliberately: not enough to make him explode, just enough to provoke my sympathy and swing me over to Gerard's side. Nothing was as superficial as it seemed, and I thought all three of us understood each other very well.

Sometimes my mother suggests that I should try just taking things at face value for a while, but how can I, when things have so many different faces?

· · ·

My mother always asks for a table for three, "but there'll only be the two of us eating." The guy who met us inside the door of the restaurant greeted Gerard by name — I thought it was like calling to like, this guy dressed just that little bit finer, handkerchief in his top pocket and studs in his cuffs — and then said, "A table for three, is it, Dr Logan?" and for a moment I could feel both of my companions glancing at me with a touch of hesitation in them.

I said nothing. I don't strike attitudes in public, unless that's an attitude in itself. Like the weather, like the poor, Small is always with us and I was pleased that they'd remembered, but he doesn't need a seat at the table.

· · ·

The menus were vast and leather-bound. *Food dressed up in a suit and tie*, I told myself, and nothing to be intimidated by. Even so, I was grateful when Kit said, "We know our way around this pretty well. Why don't we just let Michael relax, while we put together a birthday feast for him?"

"Yes, of course — so long as it is a feast for Michael, not for Kit. Which means that we leave here with our tastebuds intact, Michael, yes? Nothing too ridiculously spicy."

"I can take it," I murmured, in reaction to the face that Kit was pulling.

"Of course you can, but there's no need. Why force yourself to eat something so hot you can't taste it? Kit's addicted to the endorphin rush, that's all. You and I don't have to cater to his addictions."

"We're all addicted to an endorphin rush," Kit said. "We just look for it in different places. I eat chillies, Michael runs; what do you do, Gerard? For the rush?"

"You know perfectly well what I do." He took his glasses off, either to clean them or else to give Kit the benefit of his uninterrupted glare. Then the well-dressed man came back with the wine list, which was even fatter than the menus. Gerard reached towards it, then drew his hand back. "No, I think probably not tonight, thank you. Tiger beer, I think, for all of us; and another five minutes with the menus, we haven't decided yet."

· · ·

A tall chill glass, brimming with amber and beaded with bubbles inside, slick with condensation under my hand: I sipped and listened to their bickering over the brinjal and the bhuna, the kofta and the keema and the kurai gosht, and felt oddly and inordinately happy. Hungry too, but that was a part of the happiness; and here came a waiter with poppadums and pickles, and that was better yet. I could sip and crunch and listen, and watch the ceiling-fans that were not turned by punkah-wallahs at all but by regular electricity, and I was quite happy to say yes when they asked if I liked seafood, and to take them on trust when they assured me that I would like spinach and okra too. I felt like I was inside the bubble, accepted, under the aegis of that suit and tie. I wasn't sure what I'd done to deserve it; a few games of chess and a dogwalker's badge didn't seem to be enough, somehow. But my mother had taught me that no one ever does get what they deserve, and if I was going to come out on the plus side of this particular equation, well, no doubt it would all balance up later.

Meantime, I could just enjoy it, food and company and ambience and all. I never had been in such a restaurant, booths that were almost private rooms, all the space we needed to be discreet. Plates came and steaming bowls and breads, and this was just the starters. Kit showed me how to eat with my fingers, straight from the dishes, while Gerard spooned himself a serving and spread his napkin on his lap and ate decorously with a knife and fork.

"You get as greasy as you like," he said generously. "I don't mind so long as you wipe up afterwards, and I'm sure they'll bring you fresh napkins and a finger-bowl; but we have cutlery, so why not use it? Why pretend to be Indian natives, when you're so transparently not?"

"Why pretend to be an Oxbridge gentleman," Kit shot back, "when you so transparently already are?"

This was an old argument, and could lead nowhere but here, entrenched positions and the battle replayed I thought for my own benefit, which was kind of them but not strictly necessary. I gave my attention to the food, lamb and fish and chicken each in its sauce, in its spices.

. . .

The main course came with a separate table added at the end of the booth, solely to support the biggest naan I'd ever seen.

"House special," Kit grinned, tearing off handfuls and passing them around while dishes and plates were whisked away and replaced with new. More meats, vegetable side-dishes that should have been a meal in themselves, rice and raita; I nibbled on the bread in my hand, gazed at the rest and wished that I could eat all night and not be full.

Right now, the bread was treat enough. Inside the soft and flaking crust I found minced meat on one side, sweet coconut and raisins on the other, and I thought perhaps I'd misjudged Gerard just as he had wanted me to. Perhaps he didn't dress to impress at all, perhaps he dressed to conceal. Perhaps we all did. Perhaps Kit was dressing me to conceal whatever it was that he thought I shouldn't show around.

A new shirt, new hair and a gaudy pair of trousers couldn't contain Small. You couldn't hide him under a bushel, he'd still shine through. Actually, I'd wondered if all this evening's dance was just cover, to make a situation where they could quiz me about Small; but they didn't ask, they didn't acknowledge his presence for a moment after that first quizzical pause at the door.

Instead, when they weren't picking at each other, they talked about Quin. Quin the professor, the rising fiery light, the savage intelligence; Quin the clubman, the doubly clubbable, white tie in London society with Gerard or leading his pack of acolytes around the student night scene here, "like wolves to the slaughter," Kit said, doing his best to look the innocent lamb. Quin the patient, the terribly impatient, bedridden and hagridden and howling to be free as he never would be again.

"He ought to be in hospital," Kit said, because Gerard clearly couldn't ever allow himself to say it, "only he made us promise not to do that, after the last time. He hates being sick, he's terrified of dying and he says that hospitals are factories for the preparation of corpses, so he won't go back. We had to promise to look after him, to help him die at home."

It seemed to me that they were doing the opposite of that, they were helping him to keep alive, fighting that losing battle in the long home of lost causes. If it didn't make them happy, perhaps it made them feel good. I played with my hair until Kit slapped my hand away, both of us quiet now while Gerard talked softly about one more Quin, Quin the lover, tender and painful and precise, and

I thought that if there should have been a fourth sat at that table, it wouldn't have been Small the empty place was set for.

. . .

Later, it seemed much later, we came back to number thirty-nine with a doggy-bag for Nigel and a fat, fizzing feeling in me at least. I couldn't speak for the others, but I had too much food in my belly, residual spices on my tongue and an airy, beery frothiness in my head. I was just composing a careful goodnight, in hopes of not having to use it yet, when Gerard told me briskly to sit down, there in the offshoot, a high stool at the high counter.

I did what I was told. He went into the kitchen, and from there into the bathroom, and so back.

Whether Kit was expecting this, whether he'd budgeted for it, whether he'd worked for it I didn't know, I couldn't tell; but Gerard came back with a large orange, a bottle of distilled water and a packet of syringes.

"I should probably ask your mother," he said, "but I'm not going to, you can do that yourself. If she says no, never mind. And I hope you never need to do this anyway, I don't ever want you to find yourself alone in here; but if you're going to be on the team — and Kit and Nigel have set this up between them, I can read a conspiracy when it licks me in the face — then you need to know how to give Quin an injection. Kit'll show you how, you sit there and practice, then I'll come back and check. I'll test you again in the morning, see if you can do it sober, but I need to be sure that you can do it drunk. Try not to jam the needle through your own finger, that's counterproductive."

Kit unwrapped a syringe, pulled off the protective cap and held it horizontally in front of my eyes.

"Sharp end, blunt end. Fill it like so ..."

I want to be on the team. I want my mother to say it's okay. I want my brother to say it's okay. I want to be a part of this. I want a reason to get up early, to stay up late. I want to eat with my fingers and drink beer from a glass, I want to sing for my supper, I don't want to be a skeleton at the feast.

I don't want to see a pear in a bottle, or blood in a syringe. I want blood in my oranges, a dead king on a chessboard, shah mat, no place else. I want to be a courtier, a parasite, a nurse. I want to drink Quin's pain, I want to grow fat on it so that he need grow no thinner. I want to give as good as I get, but I don't know how. I want to outreach myself, to be better than they expect, to be more. I want to be greater than the sum of my parts ...

VIII

BEING SMALL

Sometimes, often, I wonder how it is that Small sees the world. He uses my eyes, sure, as his own can only see through glass, and that darkly. But does he, can he, would he want to see what I see? I think not, he'd find it jarring.

Eyes are just the optics, that give good measure of what patterns of light come their way. It's the mind that sorts and shuffles, adds meaning, understands. In every way that matters, then, it's the mind that does the seeing. Small's mind is a closed book to me, like last year's diary closed and locked away, all the writing in it long since done. Unchanging, unchangeable: stroppy little mannikin, what does he truly make of all these data I supply, what world has he built in his little head to contain them?

It's easy to turn him into metaphor, easy and false. He can be a pupa caught forever short in his metamorphosis, the imago that never was, cocooned *in vitro* and perpetually baffled by this adult insect world: all bright colours and sharp edges and rough raw sounds, how is he ever to understand it who never had the chance to live in it? Like an alien I can see him squatting in his spaceship bottle, on his universal shelf, watching and not sharing whatever goes on beyond his cupboard cosmos. If he took notes, it would only be a way of recording his own bewilderment. He can't learn from us, from me, from what I do; he doesn't have the capacity.

On another day he can be the puppet-master, the spider squatting in the centre of his web with a leg on every string and all the strings attach to me, so that he twitches and I jump, how high he has determined. All my choices are his own, I dance for him who cannot dance at all. And speak for him, and eat for him, and all my body is just him, out there distance-learning in the world. I am his periscope and his torpedo both, his prosthesis. Wonderful what they can do these days for the disabled.

Or he can be my cold and unreachable heart, the figure in my carpet, the ghost in my machine; or he can be my saviour, my criterion, *deus ex machina*, the point of my perspective. Or the sign and symbol of my mother's hand in mine, the control she keeps over me, how she displaces any focus else: so long as Small is the mote in my inward eye, then how can I turn my gaze elsewhere, outside the family, away from her?

Analysis breeds paranoia. What's the point? He is not a metaphor, for my use or anyone's else. He is my brother, my twin, my mother's other son. He is himself, in his jar and in my head, in my heart, in my life. If I have to live a second life on his behalf, if I have to divide my time between us, I won't complain at that.

But I would like to know the way he sees things. The way he sees me, I suppose, and what I do. We don't talk any more, the way we used to. It's like living in a silent movie: we sleep together and eat together, we share books and walks and party invitations when they come, but we can't have conversations. The most we can do is mouth at each other like fish in deep water, gesticulate wildly and hope that someone walks on with a caption to spell out what we mean.

It's bad, when you need someone else to interpret between your brother and yourself; worse, when your brother can't or won't talk to anyone but you. Never mind my mother's claims to understand, she knows nothing. I am the world's living and only expert on Small, and I don't pretend to follow the convolutions of his mind. All I know is this, that he and I are poles apart, but opposite poles attract. We cling like magnets and redraw all the world around us like patterns in iron filings, dance and twist in filigree, in tandem, he in his small bottle and I in mine.

IX

CHEMOTHERAPY

I want to lose a game *of chess. I want to lose a friend. I want him to go gentle into that good night, no more raging. I want the night to be good to both of us. I want to say good night, God speed, and mean it; I want him to wish me well. I want to wish him well, but I can't do that.*

I want to be stronger than I am, but I don't want to grow into my strength. I don't want to grow at all, I don't want to be big. I want to be small. I want to be Small. Shock horror, but I do. Not Small-in-a-jar, a shrill acid gnome in vinegar, never that; I want to be Small-as-he-is, in my head and heart, in my belly, bedded down, the one with the easy ride. I want to be the eunuch in the harem. I want to be carried around, I want to watch, I want to criticise, I never want to do anything. I never want to have anything to do. I never want to have to lift a finger.

I don't want to be responsible. I don't want to be the butterfly, living with the knowledge of the storm.

I don't know what I want, but it isn't this:

where I sit in the dark and feel as though I'm breathing for the house, for the whole house and everyone who's in it, which amounts to me and Quin. Not Small. I don't bring him here any more, or else he doesn't come.

Unless he lurks, of course, unless he just squats in the shadows and listens in and never lets me know that he's around. That's always possible. Maybe he's graduated, poltergeist to stalker. Maybe they're two facets of the same thing, the jewel in the head of the toad. There must be something about him that shines; maybe I should be grateful, to be so thoroughly watched over.

If I am. It only feels like that sometimes, and I try not to go down there. I've got another life, other lives to live now, and I don't need Small scratching at my shoulder, dribbling down my neck. I don't need to feel supervised, accompanied, shared.

I don't know what I do need; it isn't that.

. . .

Quin has good days, good nights, and this is one of them. He's been sipping water on and off all through my shift, so I haven't needed the port in his arm, where we can put him on a saline drip. He doesn't eat any more, there's another tube we feed him through, straight into his stomach; he took that too, and kept it down, which is big on the good-news front. It's dreadful when he pukes, messy and slimy and difficult to deal with, it goes all over the tubes and the medical kit where everything's supposed to be sterile. And it hurts him, and then he's difficult to deal with, and I hate to call for help, like I can't cope with someone being sick. I'm always tense at dinner time, and for an hour after.

Sometimes he pukes blood, great gouts of it, thick and black, direct from his liver to the light. Then it's okay, it's compulsory to yell. Some things nobody has to handle on their own. Needs one to hold Quin up, one to hold the bucket; that's a minimum. And still two of us afterwards to get him clean and quiet and settled again, drifting on a diamorphine drip. We're not really supposed to have diamorphine, but Quin has friends all over, and more than one of them has a prescribing pad. I'm not allowed to touch the stuff, we keep all the hard drugs in a locked strongbox and they won't give me a key, but that's cool. I guess that's cool. It's the price I pay for being young, not big enough, punching above my weight. I don't belong here, I don't deserve this; I'm still grateful that they let me through the door.

So's Quin, or so he says. He still says so, when he's up for talking. Not that often now, but this has been a good day. We even had him raised up a little earlier, his eyes open for a while. I don't think he can see that much now, but he likes to look, and he likes to look alert. So we bathe his eyes with glycerine, that helps; and he's very good, he doesn't complain when they hurt him. He just lets them close and keeps on talking so that we know he hasn't drifted far, not too far, not out of touch.

He can't manage the board any more, even with me moving the pieces, he doesn't have that much focus; so we play chess in his head. Gambits, mostly. All the classic openings we play, he says to make sure that I know them. We don't often get to the endgame. Too much history, too many choices: he can't hold it all together, he loses grip and it all frays away from him and then he's gone again, somewhere unreachable. Or else he's hiding. Sometimes there are tears on his cheeks, and I bring out the glycerine to cover for him.

He hates this. He never says so, but I know. We all know. Stubborn but weak, it's the worst, and he overdoes both. It's the back end of charisma, the shadow-state, a kind of proud and desperate helplessness. He tries to cling, and his own personality is all he has to cling to, and even that's not really there anymore. It's paper-thin, the shell of memory when the core has gone, and his own shaking hands rip and tear at it like a clumsy child breaking what he most wants and the acid sweat in his fingers, that does damage too, and his bedclothes and his breath just reek of bitterness and rot. The bedclothes we can change, we do that once or twice a day, but the breath is harder to approach. He won't lie still to have his teeth cleaned, and some days he can't manage a spit in any case, but I'm not sure that hygiene is the issue. I think what we smell is what he breathes, what he sees, where he finds himself; and I don't know who he is out there but the place is rank and swampy, built on loss.

I don't think he knows who he is out there. I think he just barely manages to keep a handle on who he used to be, and that's the worst of it, those times that he remembers.

Sometimes he tries, though, he does try, and sometimes he has a good day, even now.

Like this:

"'S dark."

"You could try opening your eyes, it's not so dark out here," though I only had the one light burning, just enough to read by: Robert Graves, *The Anger of Achilles*. The book was his. I was working my way through his shelves, his tastes, his life in stories. In translation, I suppose. "Do you want to do that, give it a try?"

"No ... No, let be. Michael?"

"Yes, it's Michael."

"You do too much of this."

Which was just what my mother said, and Adam, and Small. All my significant others for once united, making common cause. But, "I like it here," I said, which was true.

"You mean it's convenient." His voice was a whisper now, but it could still be sharp.

"That too."

"For whom?"

"Everybody."

Dry and thin as they were, his snorts were yet expressive. I listened to this one, and flinched.

"No, truly. Listen, Quin. Everyone works, except for me. They need to sleep, if they're not actually working a night shift. Me, no school, no job," *you are my job*, they told me that, "it makes sense for me to do this. And I'm a teenager, I'm naturally nocturnal —"

"— And you're here in the daytime too, as often as not."

"Well. I said, I like it. As a library, this house is better than the Bodleian. The books aren't all lined up on parade, in proper order. They can talk to each other, you have shelves that are a conversation in themselves. That's good for me; it's all about connectivity, and that's what I do."

"What you do ... What do you do, Michael?"

"I study, I suppose."

"Yes, but what? And why? What will you do with it all, when you've learned it all?"

He was asking impossible questions, which he knew. I could have thrown them straight back: *What did you do, Quin, and why? And where did it all go, because there's next to nothing left here, just a voice that breaks and a mind that slips its gears and can't get up the hill...?*

But I don't do cruelty, I never did, and I'm not so good at dodging questions. Even the impossible ones. I said, "I won't ever learn it all. You know that, you're teasing me. It's about understanding, how people work and what we're doing here. Where we've come from, what we've built and how to look at that, how to read it, how to understand what people think."

"Is that important?"

"Yes." And then, in the silence after, because I really wasn't sure, I temporised. "To me, it is."

"Why? Why to you?"

"Because of what I am, who we are, the two of us. Because I have to think for two, for Small and me."

"Small is dead, Michael."

"Yes, I know. That's the point. He used not to be. He used to be alive, inside me; and then they cut him out and he died, and I need to know what that means, and what I can do with it. I can't just blunder around shitting and fucking like some Neanderthal before the obelisk arrives, counting on Prometheus to steal fire for me. I owe it to both of us, Small and me, I have to do better than that."

"Oh, Christ. You're looking for enlightenment."

Of course I was, I thought that was inherent; but, "Isn't everybody?"

"Actually not. A lot of people out there are content with the shitting and fucking aspects. Aren't you a little young to see the world that sharply?"

"So they tell me. Too much reading, I guess," which was purely a lie, too well practised to evade. I didn't guess, I knew, and the truth lay entirely the other way, which was why I tried never to tell it. We're born sharp, and time is blunting; the world takes our edge away. Adult company grinds us down, but they really don't like to hear that. When you're a child, every adult that you talk to is trying to teach you something, and in the process rubbing away at what you've got. That's why I was in such a hurry, to have things sorted in my mind before the people who loved me best could make an idiot of me.

Books too, books are blunting, all that mass of knowledge. Every sentence is a thread that wraps around the sweet blade of the mind. Every fact is a limiting factor, the death of possibilities. I knew it, I could feel it, I was trying to outrace the rising sun by running easterly, defiantly into the dazzle. I still had my hidden advantage, though, my secret strength. I still had Small. Small who'd never learned to read, Small who dwelt in death and talked to me and me alone, unencumbered by any adult conversation. Sharp as a hypodermic needle, Small. Hollow and sharp as he should be, as he was made to be. Even as I lost my own edge, I could still depend on Small's.

Even Quin wasn't fit to hear that. Especially Quin, perhaps, who had given his life to teaching and thought me the last of his many pupils, thought that I would always speak of him as mentor. Perhaps I would, if he was the man who closed me down, who cut away my choices till there was only the one path I could follow, broad and clear and well-intentioned all the way.

"Read to me," he said. "What are you reading?"

"The Iliad, I guess."

"In the original?"

"No. I've never looked at Greek."

"You should. Have someone show it to you, don't learn it from a book. But if you're not reading the original, you're not reading Homer."

"No. Graves. *The Anger of Achilles*. It's one of yours."

"Of course it is. Read to me."

We did this often when he grew tired of talking, when perhaps he felt himself a little start to slip. We used to keep a book beside his bed with the place marked, where we'd got to. Not any longer. He couldn't manage a whole book any more, any more than a whole game of chess. The others might read him a newspaper feature, an article, perhaps a short story; I always thought that was a mistake, to offer him anything that ended. To me he seemed happier just to share a part of someone else's journey, wherever I happened to be in whatever I was reading, to feel the run of words like a string pulling through his fingers until he lost it, until he let it fall.

"I'm just at 'The Catalogue of Ships'," I said, simply to see him smile. It wasn't true, I'd been there an hour ago, but I could turn back quietly. He'd grown to like lists, details, a world expressed by its taxonomy. The looser his own grip, the more he liked to think of things tied down, measured, recorded and defined. One time I'd been reading the King James, and nothing could have made him happier than the first book of Chronicles, the lineage of a nation spelled out in all its generations, all those long chapters of begats.

. . .

"And that's what you call a good day, is it?"

Adam, hot and stroppy, neglected for days and not pacified by this promised Saturday, his temper neither burned out on a long hard ride up the Evenlode to Charlbury nor soothed by my being mounted on Kit's spare racer, a better bike than his.

"Yes. Yes, it is." We lay scorched and sticky on spiky grass, in spiky sunlight above the river, the bikes and us all sprawled out where we'd dropped. We had one bottle of water between us, literally in the grass between us like a peace offering, except that neither one of us was offering either to pass or to use it. I stared up into the summer's glare and wondered if you could have a white kind of darkness, if that was where Quin was headed, where his eyes were taking him.

"What, sitting in the dark reading out troopship

manifests from an ancient war that certainly never happened that way if it ever happened at all?"

If I'd been sitting in the dark I couldn't have read anything, but this would have been a dangerous time to say so. I took the other track, as usual, straight into the tidal rush. "That's right. You just don't get it, do you?"

"No, I don't. That's what I'm saying, I just don't get it. So explain it to me, why don't you? I'm all ears."

All ears and a closed mind, slammed shut against temptation; but, "Actually you're not," I said, "you're all skin and sensitivity. It's Quin who's all ears, pretty much, there's precious little else left to him now. We can even take his pain away, but then his focus goes too, so he can't really think any more. He's breaking down, he's fragmenting. If he manages a lucid hour, it's getting to be unusual; if we can keep him conscious for half a day, then that's a good day."

"Good for you, or for him?"

"I don't know. I'm not sure about either. It's a victory, that's all, a day won back. I don't know if anyone enjoys it. When he's lucid, he knows what's happening to him, and he hates it. That's all the passion he's got left. And he's terrified of what comes next, the real disintegration. That's why he likes to listen to lists of things in order. It's just something to set against the chaos."

"If he's that scared, isn't it the, you know, the lucid times he should be scared of? I was him, I'd be looking to let go."

"He says we're too young, we haven't learned to value what we've got. Truth is, what he's really scared of is dying.

Being dead. When he's switched on, he can watch it coming closer, and he dreads that; but when he's off, then it's
like he *is* dead, except that he comes back on again. So it's
like he's dying again and again, every sleep is another taste
of death and it leaves him gasping, gagging every time. He
says we'll learn. I say we learned long ago, Small and me,
I've been carrying a dead one around with me all my life,
all Small's afterlife, there's nothing I don't know; but he
says he doesn't have a brother to carry him around. So he
depends on his friends, he says, to look after him in this
life, it's the only one he's got with nothing after and he
doesn't want to leave it any sooner than he has to. So we
do, we look after him, as long as he hangs in there; but
fuck, he's scared. And so's Gerard, so are Kit and Peter,
all of them, I think."

"Everyone's out of step except our Michael. Nurse
Michael, the scourge of the bedpans." But he reached a
long arm out and found me, found my neck, slipped a
finger under the chain and hooked it, twisted it, tightened
it like a choker. I gathered we weren't fighting any more.
If it hadn't been so hot we'd have been wrestling, trying
to roll each other into the nettles. Lacking that chance
to lose gracefully, stingingly — every separate swelling
a token of forgiveness, boy-style — I lay still and let him
strangle me a little, waiting for what would follow.

"Wanna get stoned, then?"

"Yeah, let's."

"What d'you fancy? I've got acid, I've got speed, I've
got some coo-ool swimmy stuff from SingKong, it's new
and I don't know what to call it..."

"Just a joint, man. We've got to get home yet, and you know what happened the last time we tried to bike high."

"No, I don't. Can't remember a thing." But he sat up with the makings in his hands and started rolling, stopping halfway only to strip his shirt off so that I could lie where I was and admire the tribal tattoo on his shoulder-blade, where his parents were least likely to discover it.

"That's what I mean. I'm like Quin, I get scared by a sudden blank." And if I was scared, how must it be for Small? Did I go away for him too, leave him stranded, or did he find himself trying to ride a whirlwind, tumbling in the dizzy chaos of a mind uprooted? I didn't know, he wasn't saying, but I'd made a lot of promises against his silence, not to let it happen again. Not until it did, at any rate. That sort of promise, recognising the inevitable but making an honest effort to hold it back for a while, at least long enough for the effort to register.

Adam grunted. There were getting to be two topics of conversation we had to avoid these days, Quin as well as Small; it didn't leave me much to talk about.

So, treading valiantly on safe ground, "Where do you get all the pills and potions from, anyway? And where the hell is SingKong?"

"Don't know much, do you? For a boy who knows everything, I mean. SingKong is a virtual city, an industrial megalopolis, all the shabby old tigers in a single brand-new shiny brand. For the ignorant among us, which is you, it just means buying stuff over the internet from anywhere in Asia. Singapore to Hong Kong, the whole nine yards, all the trading nations. That's where my best deals come from."

"What, all that spam that wants to sell us Viagra, you mean it's for real?"

"Not all of it. No pill out there's going to make your cock bigger. Sorry, and all that. But you can get prescription drugs, yeah. Easy. And it's legal."

"Can't be."

"True, it is. Here they're prescription only, but you buy them mail order from overseas and they're yours. Customs can't touch you for it, nor can the police."

"How do you pay for them, though?"

"Oh, if you want to pay, just set up an account. You're over sixteen, that's legal too, and credit's cheap."

"But...?"

"But scamming it's more fun. Other people's credit cards. I'll show you. Why, what do you want?"

"Oh, nothing. I was just curious, is all. It's really not my field, you're the man. How's that joint coming?"

"We have ignition. Lift-off will ensue. Pure Dutch skunk, this, you're going to love it."

"Oh, Christ. We'll never get back."

"Sure we will. There's a bus, I checked. D'you think I'm stupid?"

"Will it take bikes?"

"Dunno, I didn't check. We can find somewhere, leave the bikes."

"No, we can't. It isn't mine, it's Kit's. I'm not leaving Kit's bike twenty miles from home."

"Just have to smoke slow, then, won't we? And pedal

easy. Or the other way around. We'll be fine. Is there a shop here? If your mouth's as dry as mine, we're going to need more water. There must be a shop ..."

. . .

I am becoming strange to my own mother, at last, after so many years of trying. It's a case of the biter bit. She always meant me to be unusual; she couldn't have borne a child of the ordinary, a pink and gurgling babe, a whining schoolboy already growing into his grey suit or his greasy overalls, a garage mechanic or an office clerk in embryo. She needed difference, someone to match or complement herself, someone to show off with. That I turned out twinned, twinned with the dead, that was just a bonus: two for the price of one, me and mini-me, ten per cent extra free. She would have made me odd in any case.

Now, though, I am too slippery for her to get a grip on what I am. Sometimes when I come in from the night shift, what is draggingly late for me is early for her as it is for the world around, the world she so reluctantly inhabits. She'll be sitting in her upright chair at the little window table, where she may have been watching the sun rise or she may have been watching for me. She watches me now, as we exchange some kind of greeting; she's not good first thing and I'm a teenager, I've been up all night, I'm either monosyllabic or my mouth is running like a river and neither one is particularly useful to her.

I'm too tired or just too young to go to bed directly.

So I slump into the sofa, and we watch each other. I might perhaps ask a question about whatever brassbound job it is that she's doing at the moment, but if I do it's only to have something to toss into the empty space between us. I'm not interested, because neither is she. She's always said that work is fuel, it powers the lifestyle, no more. Specifically, she does what work she does to keep us in the manner that we have made our own — and by 'us' she means Small and me, she says. She says that often, or variations on the theme. She's not a martyr, not a sacrifice, but a driving force for sure; she sees herself as the motor, she says, while it's us who steer the boat.

Well, maybe so. She built the boat, though, she trained the crew; she chose the river and drew the maps. Theologically speaking, God's just the engineer and each of us gets to play captain. It's still God's world, God's rules and ultimately God's responsibility. Free will's an illusion and choice is a three-card trick, you choose where you're directed to choose, where you're driven to it.

She likes that, my mother. She's always been comfortable setting up my choices for me. And now somehow I've got ahead of her and she's off-balance suddenly, unsure of me, confused. She doesn't understand what I'm doing, with my time or with Small's.

Like this:

"You look tired."

"Uh-huh." Well, I would, wouldn't I? Sleep is a luxury, and I didn't have time to indulge. Put it another way, I'd been up all night and most of the day before, the night before that. I wasn't counting hours. I wasn't counting anything or costing anything, just doing whatever was there to be done.

"You shouldn't let them use you this way, it's not good for you. You're still growing, you need to spend your nights in bed. In your own bed," because she still wasn't really sure that I was being truthful here, that my nights really were spent beside a sickbed. Me and a houseful of men, without Small to watch over me: she worried that I might be sleeping with one of them, with a variety of them, with the whole transient population as it passed through.

It's interesting how people, mothers particularly, will find entirely the wrong things to worry about.

"I'm not sure I am," I said. "Still growing, I mean." I stretched out and gazed at my feet, not far enough away. "Kit weighs and measures me at the gym and I haven't grown in six months, upwards. I think I stuck at this."

Outwards, inwards, every otherwards I was growing fine. They'd clubbed together to buy me a membership — though I thought Gerard had done most of the clubbing — and Kit and I did circuits together three times a week. I still ran, and sometimes I had company then too, though I'd settle just for Nigel. Adam and I cycled when we could, not often enough but absence kept us hungry. I'd never been so fit; my life had never been so populous.

"You could still put on a spurt. Be a late developer, why not? You've tried the other thing, walking early and talking first. Just wasn't me you were talking to, you and Small always had your own language. So good for you, so much stimulation so young, I didn't have to do a thing to help. You two did it all, you practically brought each other up. I often wondered, did you share your dreams? Back when he was alive, I mean?"

"I don't know," I said. "I don't remember."

"No, of course not; but he might. You might ask him sometime."

I might. Forgetting's not my thing either, just that babyhood's an exception; my records don't go back so far. Actually I don't think anyone ever truly forgets, they just mislay the information. Forgetfulness isn't a delete function as far as I can see, it's only bad indexing and broken links.

But we'd talked about all of this before, and I thought something more was coming, and I was too tired to play games. Maybe this was how Quin felt inside: his fingers slack on the pieces, his hands sliding off the board. Except that he must feel this way every day, all the time, and always would for all the time that was left him.

I waited, and she produced her killer question. "How does your brother feel, about you spending so much time in that house, and being so tired otherwise? You only come home to sleep, how fair is that?" Except that the real question was *how do you think your brother feels* etc, and that made it not really a question at all. It was an accusation, and I really didn't need to answer it. Just as well, as I didn't have an answer. *I haven't asked, and I don't care* — not a possible thing to say, to my mother.

So I just shrugged and sat there, the very image of sullen adolescence; and after a while she stepped back, as she had to. She said, "All right, love. How is your friend, anyway?"

And I said, "Quin? He's dying," but I said it softly where it could have been vicious, it could have been another accusation flinging back. No point in that. It was just what I always said, it was always true; dying was a steady state with Quin, so question and answer were more or less meaningless. I might equally well have said, "He's fine," the way I always did about Small if anyone asked. Kit did ask sometimes, teasingly, except that I wouldn't be teased.

And then even the shrugging and the muttering became too much for me, and I settled for just sitting with my eyes closed, not really listening any more when my mother spoke; and then I was dreaming and then rousing from a dream, rousing to an empty room and sunlight on the table to show where my mother had gone, where she had left one of her Moleskine notebooks behind.

And when I picked it up it opened as they do, to the page with the rubber band snapped around it; and she'd sketched me as I slept, and it was like a confession, she might as well have written it down in capitals, stood up at Mothers Anonymous and said it aloud, *My name is Alice Martin and I don't understand my teenage son.*

Her sketching was usually neat and quick and precise, the pin through the butterfly. This was hesitant, anxious, troubled. She had my features, my body in proportion, the stretch and slump of me across the sofa, but I thought she'd missed me altogether, seen me and not known me.

It might have been the portrait of a stranger, or she might
not have known at all what she was looking at, the butterfly gazing at the caterpillar and wondering what it was,
bloody hell, all she'd done was lay a bloody egg…

· · ·

Singkong is also the Malay word for cassava. I found
that in independent research. It's amazing what you can
find, if you only go looking.

You are what you eat, you are what you wear; you are
what you read online, maybe. Maybe you are, at least. Not
me, I'm not that gullible. I just take what I want, what I
think I might find useful.

Sometimes I get it delivered.

· · ·

You're never alone with a Strand. You're never alone
with a good book. I'm never alone, full stop.

Quin, though: Quin can't smoke any more, and he
can't read, though there's always someone here to do the
reading for him and there's plenty of books. I don't think
that stops him being alone. There's always someone here,
sure, but he doesn't always know it. He doesn't always
know us, now. Sometimes he gets scared, just by our
voices. Sometimes he strains an eye open and squints at
us, all dry and shrunken, and his hands pluck fitfully at
the covers — floccillation, that's called, if you ever need
the word for it: or carphologia, that's a true synonym;

or crocydismus, that's another — and his thin pinched mouth maybe shapes words at us and he might be saying *who are you?* or he might not, he might be mumbling syllables at random and it really doesn't matter because what he means is clear enough. He's frightened and alone in a roomful of strangers, he doesn't know what's happening, he has no control. Perhaps he remembers other days, when none of that was true. Perhaps not. Again, it doesn't matter. He is here now and this is what he's doing, and you could call that being alone.

Or you could wait a while, and there comes a time when he doesn't know who he is himself, or that he has a body to inhabit. You can see that, look, I'll show you, it's like this: when his fingers twitch and there's a shudder in his skin and his breath comes fast and shallow, and you wish he could be asleep and dreaming and you know there's no chance of that, so you talk to him but that's nothing, it's meaningless, and his eyes will not be opening this hour because he's forgotten that he has eyes, there is nothing but the little candle of his consciousness lost in the long darkness, a questing where there is nothing to be found or known, and the word for that is despair if ever you should need it, but the feeling and the foundation of it, the definition is entirely being alone.

Or you could wait a while longer, sometimes it really is a long wait now, until he comes entirely back into himself, and the eyes are his and the voice is his and what they say between them. And this is the worst of it, for him and for us too. Because he smiles at us and he speaks to us and he tries terribly hard to be Quin, even if it's only

Quin the patient and much reduced from anyone he used
to be; but Quin never was alone, he never lived or slept
alone, he never went alone to work or party. And now he's
there in his big high hospital bed and that's a statement in
itself, a strong metallic tubular bell of a statement, long
and bright and sonorous, *this was bought for you and no
one else to share, where you can lie alone*, because there
are two worlds in that one room and he inhabits one and
we the other, and there is no sharper way to say that he's
on his own now. His friends are here about him and his
partner too, and we all of us only serve to stress how very
much alone he is and going solo.

Sometimes I feel most guilty, being most young and
probably furthest from him, but in truth it's himself that
makes this hard for him. When he's most himself, he's
most aware of what's happening, where he's been and
where he's going, how he has to get there. He knows when
he's been raving, he knows when he's been lost entirely,
he may perhaps have some ghost memory of each. And
he knows there will be more of each to come, and less of
this. Ultimately he knows there will be nothing, and that
for him is worse than either. He can lie there and savour
his own dying, feel the slow determined tread of it, chart
every separate step he's yet to take. This terrifies him, but
not so much as what follows, that logical final step, the
being dead.

If he were further gone, if he were raving altogether
or else lost altogether, then all this might be easier. I
might forget how scared he is of extinction, where to me
it seems so much the better choice if I could make it for

him. Without his craquelure eyes and creaking voice to remind me, I might persuade myself that there's a mercy yet in simple death, where I have no hope at all of ever persuading him.

. . .

My mother on her morning shifts, she always left before the post arrived. Not me. Late home last night or early in, whatever today might promise or threaten or withhold, I could still be sure to be around to greet the postman, to open to his knock if what he carried needed signing for or simply wouldn't fit through our letterbox.

It was a handy habit to acquire. My mother knew what cash I had, it was what she gave me; she didn't always see where it went. Sometimes she asked, "What do you do with it all, for God's sake? Tell me you're not stashing it against a rainy day, tell me you haven't got a savings account. You're not seventeen yet. I know you can't get rid of things, but surely money's different...?"

Money was different, and I could assure her so. For once I couldn't blame Small, I couldn't say "I give it all to Small, I don't know what he spends it on," even she wouldn't buy into that; but I could mumble and turn my head away, I could let her find the odd brown-paper wrapping and perhaps a foreign stamp, and that was good enough. I was sixteen, after all. Of course I'd buy porn on the net, what red-blooded boy would not? And of course I wouldn't let my mother find it.

. . .

Running with Kit on a Sunday afternoon, this is serious work; we'll do seven or eight miles around the city's rivers, he says he's training me up for a half-marathon. We don't take Nigel. Nigel is not serious.

Kit is not always serious, but he can be. So can I.

So we run, and this is not jogging; it's a steady lope, a wolf-pace that we can keep up easy as it eats the distance that we do, that makes us both confident of more. Which is the thing about Kit altogether, that wherever he takes me, whatever we do, he always makes me confident that we can go further and do more. If you'd asked me when we met, that day in the woods, of the two I'd have picked Peter as my likely friend: older and more comfortable, less edgy. Even despite Adam I'd still thought I would gravitate upwards, towards my mother's generation, always wanting to be bigger than I was.

So Kit is a surprise to me, as Adam was before; and he's a challenge and a temptation, a snare but never a delusion. No one is more real than Kit, or ever could be.

So we run his course, towpaths and bridges, like a thread that stitches all the city together despite its dividing waters; and then we head home and just before we get there we duck into the park for a lap of hard running, a race around the fence and first to touch the old oak wins an acorn. This particular challenge, sometimes, I can win it. Never in the gym, we only pretend to compete there;

twenty-four can lift more than sixteen, that's just biology. Running gives me a chance, even if it's only a chance to cheat.

Then I play dog-boy and fetch Nigel, and we do a lap of jogging, stretching, doggie-wrestling and throwing sticks. Maybe we talk now. Talking's often good, when you're hot and sweaty and cooling down.

Then back to the house and into the bathroom, under the shower together and he washes my back if I'll wash his, and then one day it's like this:

Water like a scalding flow of glass, enfolding me like a bottle, like time gone liquid, the flow and the drag of it over my skin and how it can beat me down, so hot, so hard it can numb me altogether and batter me out of my body almost, out of any sense of myself; and how it hammers on the back of my neck and the heavy run of the water downwards is counterweighted somehow by a shivering rise in my spine, a tingling that is neither warm nor chill but fierce and focused, that climbs in pulses like fists to the base of my skull and then dissipates like bruises, and it's all about possession, personality, *this is me* and *this is mine...*

. . .

"Are you done, then?"
"Yeah, I'm done."
So he shuts the shower off, and I just stand there for

a second or two, running my hands across my scalp, as if I were squeezing the water out of my hair except that there's no hair there now, Adam's sister is shaving our heads this month so that we're bald and beautiful together, cheap on shampoo; and when I blink my eyes open again Kit's looking at me through the steam, and I say, "What?" and it's a real fight to keep it light, to sound amused and nothing more, not sullen or embarrassed or flirty when I could somehow be feeling all three of those at once.

"Oh, nothing. Just you. God, if I could bottle you ..."

"Well, you can't," sudden and harsh and inappropriate.

He quirks an eyebrow at me and says, "Well, no. But if I could, I'd make a fortune. Essence of Boy, the pure thing, unadulterated."

"Essence of Scar, more like," I say, glancing down in a major misdirection.

"Oh, the scar's all part of the charm. Every boy should carry a scar or two. You just take it over the top, as usual. What, you wouldn't want rid of it, would you?"

"No. No, I wouldn't," and not such a misdirection after all.

"That's good. Be a shame to waste a feature on some-one who wasn't grateful for it. Michael, you will let me know when you're ready to hit the clubs, won't you? We'll rustle you up some ID, get you through the door, and then it's downhill all the way. Everyone is so going to love you."

"Thanks, but I'm loved enough already."

"You say that now. Give it another year, for the other shoe to drop. And then just let me be there when it happens, yes? I want to watch. Now play towel-boy for us, there's a sweetie; then you go and sit with Quin a while, and I'll see what's cooking in the kitchen."

And double it, he means, or put a pan of rice or pasta on the boil to go with, just for us. No one in that house ever ate enough, or thought we really needed more. We burned carbohydrates like coke in a furnace Sundays, gym days, pretty much every day. Sometimes it was easier just to take him home with me, my mother understood about starving age but feeding adolescence; except that then I'd have to put up with questions, teasing, who knew what. That could go on for days, and it never felt the easier choice at all, in retrospect. Best days were when we did the cooking ourselves, or else went out for fish and chips.

. . .

Dressed and damp, fresh and weary and alert, sipping water and fizzing with endorphins, I sit and watch Quin's breathing, timed against the steady drip of saline through his port. I do this often at times like these, when I'm too hyped to read. It brings me down gently, it tunes me in with Quin's day and where he stands within it. Slow and shallow, he's asleep, if sleep is the proper word these days, I'm never sure. Sharper, faster but still steady, he's dreaming, or what we've chosen to interpret that way, like Nigel when his paws twitch and he's snoring and we say he's chasing rabbits.

When there's a break in the rhythm, a sudden silence or a sudden gasp, that's when I know that Quin's awake.

When he's suddenly tentative, unsure about his breathing or his body, what's going to hurt and how much.

"Hey," I say softly, just to test the water.

His lips move just a fraction, just enough. I reach over to touch them with the mouth of my bottle, test the water another way, see if he wants a drink — and catch myself just in time, I've been so shouted at for doing that, so threatened, *we won't leave you alone with him if you can't be trusted.*

So I draw my bottle back, one more thing that Quin is not allowed to share, and find his own bottle on the side table, and hold that for him to suck at. Which he does; and then he moves his mouth and forms his breath into shapes, into spiky whispered words; and I lean close to hear him and he says,

"Rook to King's Bishop six."

He always used to call them castles, but since talking grew harder he's converted. We both use the old notation, by dint of childhood training in his case and learning from classic texts in my own, so no problem there. The only problem is that he's offering me a mid-game move and he and I are not in the middle of a game, we haven't played for weeks and then it was desultory and soon abandoned. I'm damn sure he's not been holding that game in his head all this time, and if he had been this move would still make no sense within it.

"Quin? Where did that one come from?"

He only says it again, "Rook to King's Bishop six, your move," and it must be important, it must matter, to be worth the effort of air that it costs him and all the slipping focus of his mind. But it can't be real in any space outside his head, and I can't join in under these conditions because telepathy is a closed book to me. So I say, "I'm sorry, I don't think I was here for the start of this one, d'you want to tell me how the pieces lie?"

We've still got his old set in the sideboard here, I could set the game up to his dictation, easier to get a grip that way; but I never imagined that he would be able to describe it and I'm right, he says "Never mind" and nothing more. A couple of dozen pieces and their places on the board, all the dynamics of the mid-game, opportunity and sacrifice and threat, all of that is way too much for Quin to keep a hold on nowadays. He's building a dream in there, a fantasy, a little focal point he can believe in, with whatever capacity for faith he has remaining; and he's trying to involve me, to give it depth and meaning.

And I'm frightened, suddenly and thoroughly. Of all the ways I'd thought an end could come, I'd never seen it here, not like this, where Quin tries to bind me to a game I can't be playing in a world that isn't mine. I can't take that. I won't let him possess me as an avatar: hollow or inhabited, either is as bad. And of course there should be nothing I can do, I can't burrow into his brain to find myself and save myself, let myself out of there in whatever strange or sick distorted form he's held me.

But neither can I shrug and smile and let it go, let myself go, down and down with Quin on this long slow spiral. If he's got me — inside his smile somewhere, behind his bleeding blinding eyes, wherever — he won't be letting me go. It's a lesson well learned from him, from his friends, from everyone who ever loved him: *Quin hates to be alone.* If he's found a way not to let that happen, to take someone with him when he goes, he'll be relentless.

And all I can do is match him in his unrelenting, stop him swift and sudden and irrevocable. Before he's got a better grip on me, while he still has only that little part of what I am that plays a little chess. Quin's mind runs wide and deep, or at least it used to. I don't know what resources he has in there that he can still tap into. Even unconsciously, maybe even when he's unconscious because I don't believe he sleeps as other people sleep, as we do, not any more. I think he could make me, keep me, take me away. And I do not want to go. I've been bottled up long enough already.

. . .

I don't have to think. I am not thinking. Someone else can do my thinking for me.

. . .

I don't even have to watch. I am not watching. Someone else can do my watching for me.

. . .

Watch. You watch. Watch this:

where all I can feel is the tremble in my fingers and

the pallor in my skin, I can, I can feel that in the dizziness and the pounding blood in my ears as I try to hold myself together unless I'm trying to pull myself apart, and vibration white finger is a joke but I'm not laughing and nor is he as we pull open the sideboard and rummage among the drugs, scattering bottles, scattering capsules and pills and blister-packs and boxes.

All Quin's major medicine, all his heavy stuff is kept under lock and key and I do not have a copy of the key. But that still leaves a bevy, a raft, a pharmacopoeia of lesser drugs and draughts and potions, plenty of prescriptions and all the over-the-counter buys of a long sickness and a team of eager amateurs with money, all the homoeopathic and herbal medicines, all the vitamin supplements and dietary aids and of course the bags of saline and the needles, the drips and feeds and plastic gloves, the sharps box in its yellow, all the paraphernalia of nursing care ...

· · ·

Where's best to hide a tree, a book, a purloined letter? Among their own kind, famously.

Our mother could look for porn, and never find it. Michael didn't need it; nor did Small, for very different reasons, though Small might have liked it better if Michael did.

What came in brown paper from uncertain SingKong origins was not hot Asian teens or exotic bondage videos in dodgy formats. Shame on her, shame on you for ever thinking that it might be.

And if these hands trembled as they reached to the back of the cupboard, as they spilled bottles and boxes out onto the carpet until they found the little ones they wanted, no blame to them for that. Anyone might tremble, such a time and such a purpose. Anyone might fight himself, pull back and press ahead. It might be war, where only the strong survive.

· · ·

He is not strong, but I am. We are. When we do not fight between ourselves.

· · ·

When we fight between ourselves, victory is to the strong.

· · ·

Out of the strong comes forth sweetness.

· · ·

If these fingers tremble as they slip a hypodermic from its wrapping, as they uncap the bottles that have come so far, invert them one by one, thrust the needle through their seals and draw the clear liquids down, tap the syringe to mix the cocktail lightly, still no blame, even to the strong. If the hypodermic drags at them, momentous — well, they ought to feel the weight of what they do. This is not weak. Nothing here is weak now.

. . .

This is us, watch us now, the man on the bed and the boy approaching. His eyes may flicker and his skin may sweat, he may breathe short and shallow from a dry mouth, but if he hesitates it isn't doubt, it's only indecision.

Through the port with the saline, an easy injection into the feed and let it drip down through the valve like a slow tide rising? Or else direct into a vein and swift away?

Youth has its urgencies, and the man on the bed has veins like flaccid cords beneath his inelastic skin. No pressure, it's habit as much as heart that keeps his bad blood trudging with its boots on, undischarged. No matter. A thumb pressed down into the forearm can raise a vein, with patience.

Can raise his eyelids too, painful and unlikely; and his voice like querulous corn in the wind, "What is it, is that Michael?"

He can't see. We can't say. Small wonder.

Easy, now. Go with it. Go away...

. . .

And he does, he does go, far and fast.

. . .

And when he's gone, then nothing more can happen, nothing must.

And so they find us, later: Quin gone and I am in a corner in the dark, afloat in my body with bottles all around me, and nothing new in that.

I know he didn't want it, but I wanted, oh, I wanted him to want it. Too bad for one of us, or else for both.

I don't know what I want; it isn't this. This is what Small wanted, he's a laughing gnome, Small always gets what he wants. Why can't I?

Because I don't know what I want, except it isn't Small. Unlucky, then. Unlucky again. We're mirror-twins, reversed. He knows how much he wants me. Ever and ever, amen.

X

BEING SMALL

I am not myself.

In fact, I realise now, I'm Small.

Always we'd assumed — which means of course that my mother had told us, and she started doing that way back when I believed her, when I could still take her on trust — that there were two twins and the strong one came out on top, on the outside, and that was me and Small could only leech off me, my little leech, my brother. And so he died and that was sad but right, as it should be. That was the great certainty of my life, that we'd got us the right way round.

Not so. She was wrong, she raised us wrong, we had lived all our lives on a lie. On an inverted world, believing north to be south and vice versa.

Small it was who was the strong one, who lived inside me, off me, on me, through me. I was his vessel, his weaker vessel, nothing more: his shell, his transport, his eyes on the world, his pasture. Dying made no difference, not to him. Except that I grew fitter, I made a better host. He was embedded already, what reason did he have to let go?

All these years I've carried him and never realised. Body and mind he had me; no wonder he didn't want to share. Except with our mother, of course. We made such a lovely family, a perfect trinity, mother and son and the wholly ghost. Wholeghost, with added grit and fibre.

He was the tough one, and he took me when he wanted to. He squats inside me somewhere like a genie in a bottle, and you only have to rub my scarred belly to make him speak. Don't do it. That way madness lies, for one of us at least.

We always were identical, but now I look a lot like him: hairless and shrunken and gazing out through glass. I stay in my room mostly, when I'm allowed. He has me to himself, the way he always wanted. We play on the ChessLord to kill time, and he wins every game.

These days, these nights I dream his dreams.

about the author

Chaz Brenchley has been making a living as a writer since the age of eighteen. He is the author of nine thrillers, most recently *Shelter,* and two fantasy series, *The Books of Outremer* and *Selling Water by the River.* As Daniel Fox, he has published a Chinese-based fantasy series, beginning with *Dragon in Chains*; as Ben Macallan, an urban fantasy series beginning with *Desdaemona.* A British Fantasy Award winner, he has also published books for children and more than 500 short stories. Chaz has recently married and moved from Newcastle to California, with two squabbling cats and a famous teddy bear.

CPSIA information can be obtained at www.ICGtesting.com
Printed in the USA
LVOW05s1833131114

413544LV00019B/1371/P